Large Print Ros
Roszel, Renee.
Bride on the loose

NEWARK PUBLIC LIBRARY
NEWARK, OHIO

GAYLORD M

BRIDE ON
THE LOOSE

BRIDE ON THE LOOSE

BY

RENEE ROSZEL

MILLS & BOON®

First published in Great Britain 2001
Large Print edition 2002
Harlequin Mills & Boon Limited,
Eton House, 18-24 Paradise Road,
Richmond, Surrey TW9 1SR

© Renee Roszel Wilson 1999

ISBN 0 263 17283 X

Set in Times Roman 16½ on 18½ pt.
16-0302-46740

Printed and bound in Great Britain
by Antony Rowe Ltd, Chippenham, Wiltshire

CHAPTER ONE

DANA CRAWLED OUT of the sea at dawn, grateful her stupidity hadn't turned her into shark *hors d'oeuvres*. Jumping off her fiancé's yacht in the dead of night might not be the dumbest thing that had ever been done in the history of the universe, but it was a close second.

The sand was white and as fine as talcum, making her hands and knees sink and slide with every attempt to move forward. Finally, *finally,* when she was sure her upper torso would be clear of sea water, she collapsed. "Don't crash now, you idiot," she muttered, one side of her face compacting damp sand. "You have to hide!"

"Hey, there!"

A man. Though instantly alert and on guard, she was too tired to lift her head. She opened her eyes and noticed a wooden dock around a distant curve of beach. A cabin cruiser was

5

moored there. Unfortunately for her, a man had just leaped off the pier and was heading in her direction. She moaned. *Run away, idiot!* she told herself. *Tate probably has his people out looking for you by now! Run!*

She pushed up on one elbow. Her arm quivered. Spending heaven-knew-how-long paddling around in the ocean took a lot out of a person. As the stranger jogged her way, she sagged down, her cheek once again meeting cool sand. Squinting into the sunrise, she couldn't tell much about his face, but he jogged like a man who'd done it before—a lot. He had a trim, strapping silhouette; purple and pink streaks of early morning light underscored the sinewy power of a great pair of long legs.

Dana, stop ogling the man's thighs and make a break for it! she commanded herself. *You didn't risk life and limb jumping off Tate's yacht just to be caught like a beached whale.*

Dana felt herself being gently lifted and turned to her side by a pair of strong hands. Her cheek no longer rested on cool sand, but was snuggled against a warm, very masculine chest. She fancied she could even hear a heart-beat. A little rapid, but solid, giving her a bi-zarre sense of protection even though he was probably one of Tate's hired thugs!

"Are you okay?"

She blinked, lifting her gaze to bring his face into focus. Even as exhausted as she was, her heart did a high kick of appreciation. For a thug, his blue eyes were appealing, and he was startlingly handsome. He was the image of those to-die-for male models in the TV ads where they do something particularly sensitive like mop a kitchen floor or diaper a baby. He had the kind of face an eyeglass frame com-pany would hire to put on a pair of their glasses, knowing that women all over the country would haunt frame shops hoping he'll drop by.

If this guy was one of Tate's men, he wasn't one she recognized. Those eyes, she'd remem-ber. But then, what did she really know about the conniving jerk she'd almost made the mis-take of marrying? She squinted, not sure what to say or do. "What?" Her voice was a croaking whisper. Maybe she'd swallowed a little too much salt water.

"I asked if you're okay." He looked concerned.

She eyed him, suspicious. *Yeah, he would want to know that. Tate couldn't pull off his little coup if I drowned.*

"How did you get all the way out here?"

"Out where?" What was he talking about? Hadn't she washed up on Miami Beach? A rather deserted part, true, but...

"This is a privately owned island."

She frowned, confused. When she'd jumped off Tate's yacht, she'd gotten a little turned around, yes, but the lights she'd seen, she'd thought...

"An island?"

He scanned her face, then the rest of her. His expression clouded and he returned his gaze almost guiltily to her face. She wondered why.

"What's your name?" he asked.

So what did she say? Even if he wasn't one of Tate's men, she still needed to hide. ''Exactly where am I?''

''This is Haven Cay in the Berry Islands.''

The Berry Islands? They were in the Bahamas! The yacht must have sailed farther off the coast of Miami than she'd realized during the big pre-wedding bash.

''Miss?'' he said. ''What's your name?''

She squinted at him, unsure what to say. She'd been abundantly dumb, leaving that note telling Tate she'd overheard his sleazy plan. If he got wind of where she was, he'd be Johnny-on-the-spot, slathering on the charm, telling her she was mistaken—had misunderstood. Not to mention her mother, so bent on this marriage she couldn't see the handwriting on the wall. She'd add to the brew, badgering relentlessly. There would be no escaping the marriage if anybody found out where she was.

Did she dare confide in this stud? Tate would offer a reward to know her whereabouts. Or was this man the one in ten thousand not motivated by greed? She smirked inwardly.

"You do know it, don't you?" he asked, drawing her back.

"What?"

"Your name." He shifted her, lifting her more into a sitting positing. She got a glimpse of the rest of herself and was shocked. Good Lord, she'd forgotten she'd shucked everything she'd had on but her bra and panties while she'd been in the water. And those lacy scraps were soaked, leaving nothing to the imagination but the brand name. Horrified, she flinched.

"Are you in pain?"

Dana shoved at his chest, dislodging herself from his arms. She fell back on the sand; her breath whooshed painfully from her lungs. For a minute the man hunched beside her had two blurry heads. She faced the fact she was more exhausted than she realized. She couldn't even sit up on her own.

With a moan, she drew a forearm over her eyes. It was as close to sticking her head in the sand as she could get.

"I'd better take a look at you." His fingers rested lightly on her head. She jerked away but only succeeded in throwing out her arms, making him visible again. He placed a hand on each side of her face and looked down at her, his jaw tensed. A swath of black wavy hair fell across his forehead, ruffled by a breeze. The lock shone like obsidian. "Don't be embarrassed, Miss," he said softly. His hands gently began to probe beneath her wet hair. "I'm a doctor."

"A—doctor?"

He nodded. A vague smile crooked his lips. She considered the smile as his hands moved tenderly, carefully, over her scalp. The expression wasn't sly or smarmy, but sympathetic. If he really was a doctor, he had a good bedside-manner smile.

Even so, she didn't dare tell him who she was. She needed a place to hide—and time. Two weeks, in fact, when she couldn't be found. By then the deadline for Tate's scheme would pass and their marriage would be worthless to him.

His hands slid down to her shoulders as he touched, probed, asked if she felt pain. She shook her head vaguely. No pain. But she felt something. His fingers grazed along her ribs, then below her navel, where he pressed gently. ''Pain?''

She met his gaze. ''No.'' Her flesh prickled at his touch and her breathing grew uneven and labored. She wondered if she should mention those symptoms, then decided they were best left unsaid—since they'd only developed after his hands had begun to explore her body.

Poor man. He couldn't help being good-looking, or that his routine checkup had a troubling seductive quality about it. She wondered if her reaction was typical of his female patients and if it caused him much trouble in the examining room. Of course, he probably had several muscular nurses at the ready to hold patients at bay when lust overcame them. Besides, he surely wore more than a pair of shorts and an unbuttoned cotton shirt during office hours.

His hands skimmed over her panties and she closed her eyes. She was afraid the groan she heard came from her throat.

"Something hurt?"

She shook her head, then decided she'd had enough. "Look, Doctor, I'm okay. Really." She dragged herself up on an elbow.

He sat back on his haunches. Whopping good haunches, if you were into men's haunches. She'd never thought she was, but being in such close proximity to really first-class haunches made her rethink. Irritated with herself, Dana pulled up to sit. "I—I'm just tired. Nothing's broken." *Except maybe my heart,* she added silently. *Tate and his shoddy, sneaky plans!*

The doctor moved to one knee, his smile reassuring. "My name's Sam. Sam Taylor."

That brief flash of teeth in the golden light held a burst of eroticism that was way over the top for your average bedside manner. She wondered if he had any idea how gorgeous he was early in the morning.

"Do you think you can stand?"

She shook her head, meaning she wasn't sure, but he took it as a no. Before she realized what was happening, he lifted her into his arms. "Well, then, I'd better carry you."

Dana swallowed hard. Why hadn't she thought of that! Well, as long as he had...

"You didn't tell me your name." He began to carry her along the beach, away from the water and his boat.

"Where are we going?"

"My great-aunt Beena's place." He winked. "It's better for resting. And Beena will have food."

Her breath caught at the effect of the brief closing of that one eye. She had to make herself start the breathing process again. Breathe in, breathe out. Repeat. "Your aunt's place?"

He seemed to carry her effortlessly. Dana could detect no hint of breathlessness as he talked. "I told you this was a private island."

"Oh right. So it's your aunt's island. Must be nice." A private island? Dana had been so muddle-headed when he'd mentioned it before, it hadn't fully registered. What better hiding place could she hope for? Did she dare think she had a chance to stay here for two whole weeks without her whereabouts being discovered? "Is your aunt sick?"

That sexy, crooked grin reappeared. "No, but I'm not her doctor."

"Why? Aren't you any good?"

Though his skin was tanned, she saw a flush of darker color tint his cheeks. How charming. He was blushing. "I've never had any complaints."

Dana just bet he hadn't. He probably specialized in young women! "You're a gynecologist, right?" She blanched. Where had *that* question come from? She was aghast that only hours after discovering the man she'd promised to marry was a liar and a phony, she could even think such thoughts about a total stranger.

He cleared his throat. "In my practice I pretty much do it all."

She was surprised, but not quite so surprised as she was to find she'd lifted her arms and wrapped them around his neck. She noticed in passing that he had extravagantly broad shoulders and wondered how he carried all that breadth around and remained upright. "Small town doctor?" she asked.

"No." He inclined his head, indicating something ahead. "There's my great-aunt's place."

Dana shifted around and caught her breath. The place looked like a Gothic castle that had managed to drag its gray granite bulk out of Transylvania and plop down in the middle of this tropical paradise. As the cardiovascularly fit doctor trudged over a sandy rise, she could see the whole amazing structure. "Wow!" She knew that sounded lame, but excused her brain-deadedness on bobbing around in the ocean for hours. An experience like that might even dumb-down Einstein.

"Mmm-hmm."

She stared at the doctor, confused. "Your aunt lives in a castle?"

He grinned. Shame on him! What if one of his young women patients had a bad heart? That smile would do her in. Since Dana wasn't in tip-top physical condition at the moment, either, in a self-defense move, she turned away to study the castle. Every gargoyle was fashioned in the shape of a cat, every spire held aloft by one. There were crouched cats, snoozing cats, leaping cats, snarling cats, running cats, prancing cats, cats in top hats, cats in ballet skirts, cats in boxing gloves.

"She likes cats?"

"How'd you guess?"

Dana faced him. He was grinning again. She sucked in an appreciative breath. "So, you live here with your aunt?"

"No, I come to visit every summer."

"You just got here?" She wondered how long he stayed, and decided to wangle the question into the conversation later.

"Just this morning."

"So, nobody's sick?"

"Not that I know of."

A shadow passed over them and Dana noticed that he'd carried her beneath a granite archway carved with frolicking cats. She looked around. They were within a stone wall that undulated with the landscape. The sand had given way to a lush lawn that led gradually upward toward the top of the low hill where the gray edifice loomed.

"Aren't you getting tired?" she asked. After all, they'd been heading gradually uphill for more than a quarter mile.

His brows pinched slightly in question. "No."

She inhaled, experiencing a charge of feminine admiration. She felt much better, all of a sudden. She could probably even walk, but didn't make the offer. He wasn't even sweating. Besides, riding in his arms was stimulating, somehow. She was surprised at how quickly her exhaustion was slipping away.

"How are you feeling?" he asked.

"Fine." She bit her lip. Stupid! Do you *want* to walk? "I—I mean, a little better."

"Good." He glanced toward the castle, then back at her. "So what was your name, again?"

It was her turn to frown. Cute doctor or no cute doctor, Dana didn't dare tell him who she was. She had to be cautious. She'd shown how stupidly naive she could be, letting Tate sweep her off her feet the way he had. If that experience taught her anything, it was to not trust too quickly.

"You do have a name, don't you?" he asked.

She blinked, shooting him a cautious look. "Uh—" She stalled. "I—of course I have a name. Don't be silly." Her mind raced. What if she pretended to not remember it? What if she didn't have a name—for two weeks? Would that help her cause? It couldn't hurt, could it?

He came to a halt, his expression quizzical. "Okay, let's hear it."

Unaccustomed to lying, she swallowed several times. Fate hadn't led her straight to this private island for no reason. Surely she was meant to be here. This private slice of ocean-going real estate was meant to be her hiding place—she could feel it in her bones.

Dana Lenore Vanover had no intention of flying in the face of Madam Destiny's decrees. Steeling herself with resolve, she made her decision. "I—I don't remember."

He studied her for a moment, looking dubious. "You're not serious."

"I'm not?" She panicked, trying to think back. Had she said something to give herself away? After all, he was a doctor. He probably knew more about amnesia than she did. He'd probably taken courses—Amnesia 101 and Advanced Amnesia. She bit the inside of her cheek. What the heck did she know about it, anyway? Something she'd seen on an episode of "ER"?

"I don't like this."

She licked her lips, then made a face at the salty taste. "You don't?" Don't panic! She told herself. Be calm. "Why—I mean, you're a doctor. Surely—surely it's not fatal—is it?" She wanted to shout, *What don't you like? What do you know that I don't? What am I doing to give myself away?*

"It's not that." His fascinating blue eyes, fringed with lots of long, dark lashes, were narrowed in either deep concern or high distrust. "It's just that I'm not equipped for this sort of thing."

She exhaled a slow relieved breath. "Oh—well, don't worry. I'm sure—I mean, don't most amnesia victims regain their memory—in time?"

He shrugged. She detected the stretch and bunch of muscle beneath her hands. "It's not exactly in my domain, being a vet."

"Well, that's okay. I'm sure with plenty of rest and quiet I'll be as good as..." Something about what he'd said nagged at her brain, and she shifted to better look at his face. "Being a what?"

The sunlight in his blue eyes sparkled like bits of sapphire. She couldn't tell if they were twinkling with amusement or if it was a trick of the light. "A vet," he said quietly.

She felt a creeping unease begin to envelope her. "I *hope* you mean you were in the army."

His lips crooked into a wry grin. "Sorry. No."

With a rush of dismay, she cast her glance down at herself. She was practically naked in this man's arms *only* because she'd been given the impression he was a man of medicine—as indifferent to examining the human body as a mechanic was to a carburetor.

Suddenly full of energy, she struggled from his arms, landing on her feet but quickly sagging to her knees. He reached for her, but she lifted a halting hand, while trying to cover as much of herself as she could with the other. "Don't — you — come — near — me — you — you — *veterinarian!*"

He straightened, looking a little put out. "Don't say it like it's dirty."

"You lied to me!" She worked at covering herself with both hands and arms, and one bent leg, as she dropped to the ground. "You said you were a doctor!"

"I am a doctor."

"For animals!" Thwarted, humiliated and furious, Dana cast out a hand. "Give me that shirt!"

He muttered something as he shrugged it off. She bet whatever it was didn't come close to the curses she was mentally flinging at him.

"Here." He held out the shirt, and it fluttered in the breeze.

She grabbed it and slung it on, pulling the front tight around her. At least it was big. She eyed him threateningly as she crouched in a mortified little ball. "You should be registered someplace—as the local pervert vet masquerading as a real doctor."

"I *am* a—"

"Do not say that again!" She fumbled with the buttons, but her hands shook so badly she couldn't get them to fasten. Drat men and their backward buttoning shirts, anyway! In frustration, she pulled the shirt close around her again and glared. "You fondled me!"

He crossed his arms over that great chest, and she gritted her teeth, hating the fact that she'd used the adjective "great" about this pervert.

"I did not fondle you. I examined you."

"Ha! That's *pervert* talk for fondle!"

"Look, you had just crawled out of the ocean, and you couldn't stand up. You needed a doctor." He exhaled heavily. "You're not that different from a dog."

"Not   that   different...*ooo-ooooh!*"
Seething, she pushed up to stand. She might
not be Miss America material, but she was no
dog! Her determination to march to the castle
was undermined when she fell on her butt.

She cringed and rubbed her backside, but
refused to look at the pervert dog doctor.

"You'd better let me help you."

"Not if you were the last man on this entire
island!"

"I'm the only man on this entire island."

She blinked, then turned to glower at him.
"Huh?"

He watched her without humor. Apparently
being called a pervert for being a veterinarian
didn't appeal to him. But he deserved it, the
rat. He'd purposely misled her!

"I said, I'm the only man on the island."

She rubbed her throbbing posterior absently.
"Why?"

He let go with that wry, crooked flash of
teeth again. It had an affect she didn't appreciate, coming from a pervert. "It cuts down on
the raping and plundering," he said.

Dana squinted in confusion, wishing she could get up and stalk proudly away. She wondered how long it would take to get her strength back. Perhaps it had been naive of her—as a librarian—to think carrying around tons of heavy books built up lots of muscle. Evidently it didn't bulk you up as much as people might think—especially librarians. She sighed. "You mean, there are only women on this island?"

"There are around thirty male cats, and a couple of the iguanas are guys."

She turned away, pulling up her knees and resting her chin on them. "Good grief. They *need* a vet."

"Excuse me?"

She closed her eyes. "I said, you're a *pervert!*"

"That's it! You're through calling me a pervert."

Dana felt herself being lifted, and struggled to get free.

"*Quit* it," he said. "You have bigger problems than having a veterinarian see you in your drawers. If you'll recall, you have amnesia."

She glared at him, her jaw clamped. He was right! She must not forget that for a second. Clutching his shirt snugly around her, she stared away from him. "I hope," she decreed through gritted teeth, "when I remember my name, I *forget* yours."

"I think I know how you got into the ocean," he muttered.

She experienced a rush of anxiety. "You do?"

He nodded, his expression a striking blend of irritation and pity. "Somebody out there got fed up with the attitude."

CHAPTER TWO

Sam carried his unhappy burden up the flagstone steps toward the double doors of the castle. By now, he was starting to notice Miss No Name's weight. Not that she was heavy, but he wasn't a weight lifter by trade. He was—apparently—a pervert.

He gritted his teeth. He was *not* a pervert. He simply wasn't accustomed to examining beautiful, nearly nude women who washed up on beaches. Even a little pruny, the woman in his arms was one premium specimen of womanhood. With her fine blond hair spread out over the sand, she had looked like a mermaid who'd shed her tail in the process of becoming human. Her lacy underthings were all but transparent, seeming more a drizzle of frothy seafoam than anything resembling clothing.

Watching her lying there on the sand like a fantasy coming to life had been the most eerie

27

thing he'd ever experienced. He'd definitely been affected by all that soft, pale skin. Damn it. Any normal, healthy man would have been.

He halted in front of the board-and-batten door, roughly the size of a billboard turned on end. "Would you mind knocking?" he asked. "My hands are full."

She gave him an uneasy look, her big green eyes sparking with some unfathomable emotion. Without a word, she turned away and rapped. His gaze roamed to her long, pale legs. He felt an unwelcome surge of lust and bit back a curse. *Samuel Taylor, you are a doctor. Behave like one! Think of her as a cat!* He'd taken care of lots of cats with eyes that color and twice that number of legs.

He could barely hear the tapping her knuckles made on the solid wood. "Use the knocker." He cleared an odd raspiness from his throat and indicated a thick iron ring near her knees.

She reached out and wagged a hand to show she couldn't reach it. "Move me closer."

He shifted so her face was practically inside the circular handgrip. She grabbed the heavy iron, but couldn't lift it. Using both hands, she managed to raise the knocker and slam it against an iron plate. After three bangs, she let go, breathing heavily. "Enough?"

"That should do it."

"You can put me down now," she said.

He noticed she didn't look at him when she said it. "Thanks for the offer." He did nothing even slightly resembling letting her down.

After a minute she peered at him. "Well?"

He shrugged. "My arms are cramped in this position. You'll have to leap out if you want to walk."

She frowned and opened her mouth to speak. A loud creaking filled the air and she jerked around. Sam couldn't hide a brief grin. He was sure she expected Lurch, the Addam's Family butler, to be standing there. Or possibly a headless ghost wielding a hatchet.

The fact that his little mermaid curled her arms around his neck and clutched as though her life depended on it, didn't escape him. He couldn't blame her. The woman who answered the door was one of the most formidable people he'd ever run across. At six and a half feet tall and built like a Buick, Eartha was intimidating, to say the least. She was two inches taller than Sam and had him outweighed by a hundred pounds. She might be standing there barefoot and wearing a kimono of purple silk, but Sam had seen her in her karate togs and black belt. He'd personally hired Eartha as Beena's security chief, and knew she could stomp any man like a bug. And being a man with no urgent desire to be stomped, Sam was glad Eartha was on his side.

''Hello, Doc,'' Eartha said, her voice higher pitched and breathier than one would anticipate from a Buick. ''We've been expecting you.'' She took a soundless step backward on the mat of woven rushes. With the sweep of a husky arm she indicated that he come inside.

He stepped into the dimly lit foyer; the scent of beeswax candles and lavender incense hit him full force. Sam never walked into the place without experiencing a feeling of being wrenched backward through time. It wasn't a bad feeling, just a bizarre one.

"Eartha, you're looking lovely for so early in the morning."

The brawny woman blushed like a sixteen-year-old.

"I'm here bearing gifts." He indicated the leggy enigma in his arms.

"Would you like me to take it, Doc?" Eartha asked.

His female cargo shifted to frown at him. "First I'm a dog, now I'm an *it?*"

"For the record, I never called you a dog— or an *it.*" He grinned at her. "I've never carried a woman over a threshold before, either. Is it a first for you, too?"

Sam sensed a slight, watchful hesitation spiced with sadness in his mermaid's expression. But when she blinked, the look was gone. "I'm bailing," she grumbled, pushing out of his arms. She landed in a crouch, then pushed up, veering sideways a step before gaining her balance. She eyed him like an anxious child who'd stumbled into something she wasn't sure she could handle. Very quickly, that expression, too, was gone. "Thanks for the lift," she murmured.

He inclined his head in a half nod. "My pleasure."

She didn't smile, her pinched expression a clear sign she doubted it. Or, if she believed him, she didn't appreciate the sort of pleasure he'd derived. *Pervert* that she thought he was.

He made himself turn to face the head of security. "Never mind her, Eartha. She's cranky. Almost drowning will do that to a person. Just point us to Aunt Beena."

The big woman swept her arm toward the rear of the sparsely furnished entry hall. On a trestle table to his left, Sam noticed a pure white cat curled atop a fat red cushion. He recognized Mr. Chan, the patriarch of Beena's feline community, oblivious to the goings-on.

"Miss Beena is having breakfast on the back patio, Doc."

"Thanks. Ask Cook to rustle up some waffles and..." He squeezed Miss No Name's shoulder to get her attention. "What would you like for breakfast?'' For some reason, he chose not to remove his hand.

''I'd love—'' She bit her lip. ''I have no idea. But I'm awfully hungry.''

Evidently her fatigue was affecting her fighting spirit. She seemed almost meek. Or was it wariness he sensed? He experienced a prick of compassion. Of course she'd be cautious. The woman couldn't even remember her name. She'd be unsettled, to say the least.

He grinned encouragingly, squeezing her shoulder again in a reassuring gesture. ''Awfully hungry's a good sign.'' He returned his attention to Eartha. ''Tell Cook we have a starving guest, and to keep food coming. If it's edible, we'll try it.''

His mermaid gave him another look and slipped from beneath his touch. In the candlelight he thought he saw tears glimmering in her eyes. His grin faded. ''Are you okay?''

She nodded, her expression glum. ''Look, I'm sorry about snapping at you...'' Her gaze trailed away, lifting to the vaulted, beamed ceiling, then to wrought-iron candle stands flanking the arched stone portal at the back of the chamber. Finally she faced him again. "If I hadn't seen your boat out there," she whispered, "I'd think I'd somehow swam backward in time."

He chuckled. "Tell me about it."

She smiled reticently. "By the way, thanks."

He experienced a stab of guilt. He hadn't been one hundred percent "detached doctor" out there on the beach. A few of the thoughts that had darted through his head might be frowned upon by the A.M.A. But, damn it, he was a veterinarian, and the problem of caring for nearly naked beauties wearing nothing but soggy lace, had never come up before. "Yeah—well, don't thank me." He cleared his throat. "Concentrate on getting your strength back."

Shoving those lewd thoughts aside, he took her elbow and steered her toward the rear entry through which Eartha had disappeared.

"Who was that woman?" she asked, her voice hushed.

"Eartha Peele. She and her twin sister Bertha are in charge of security."

"There's another one like her?"

He nodded. "Except instead of wearing her red hair back in a ponytail like Eartha, Bertha wears hers in a bun on top of her head." He couldn't help chuckling. "Looks a little like she has a dip of orange sherbet melting on her head."

Her lips twitched, and that made him feel good for some reason. "They break bricks with their foreheads, and do some pretty fancy needlepoint. Eartha and Bertha are a couple of Renaissance Buicks."

His little mermaid didn't react this time. She merely gaped as he led her along a serpentine route through lavender scented hallways. He could tell she felt disoriented. She'd not only lost her memory, but the castle, with off-white plaster walls hung with rich textiles, was an amazingly faithful medieval recreation. She had to be hoping she'd wake up and everything would be back to normal—including the century.

After a few silent minutes Sam tugged his reluctant companion out a door into bright morning sunshine. The flagstone patio where they stood was alive with cats. Some relaxed in shady spots, some groomed themselves, some cavorted, playing chase-and-tumble. A gurgling tiered fountain fed a stony waterfall that splashed and swirled into an Olympic-size pool below the patio.

This was Sam's great aunt's favorite spot, with its view of a golf-course green perfect lawn and extravagant plantings of blooming roses and myriad tropicals. More cats, large and small, frolicked on the vast grounds. Palm leaves high in gracefully curved trees stirred with the whisper of a warming breeze. Off in the distance the ocean was visible, gleaming like antique glass.

Sam was accustomed to the sights, scents and sounds, but he could tell Miss No Name was gaping, though her face was turned away from him. He grinned at her reaction as he pulled her toward the petite elderly woman sitting at a wrought-iron table in deep shade.

His great-aunt Beena looked the same as always, her short hair standing out like a radiant corona of wispy gray. A chunky diamond broach shaped like a cat sparkled from the breast of her cotton shirt.

A skinny orange cat leaped up on the table. Beena leaned forward so the cat could clamber onto her shoulder, becoming a limp and happy fur collar. Stroking the kitty's rump, Beena turned and waved, then stilled, squinting. She grabbed a pair of rhinestone studded glasses hanging from a chain around her neck, and slid them on. She went stock-still and stared. Sam didn't blame his aunt for her surprise. He had begun very few visits with bedraggled female casualties in tow—at least not human females.

"Well, well, Sammy, love." She shooed a black cat off her lap, picked up her napkin and patted her lips. "You've always had a soft heart for strays, but when did you start collecting the two-legged kind?"

He laughed at her quick recovery. "I've been fishing, Aunt Beena. When I caught this angelfish, I decided not to throw her back."

The blonde glanced his way. "This is Beena McQueen." He moved to the table and bent to kiss his great-aunt's cheek. "The woman I love most in the world."

Beena chortled. "And why not, Sammy?" She patted his cheek. "One comes by perfection so rarely." She kissed his cheek, then shoved at his chest. "Enough mush." Beena turned her attention to the blonde leaning heavily on the table. "Who's this pretty little stray?"

Sam's mermaid held out a hand. "Hello, I'm—" Her fledgling smile faded abruptly. She peered at Sam, then glanced back at his aunt. "I—mean…"

She shook her head and stuck her hand out further. "It's nice to meet you, Mrs. McQueen."

"It's Miss." She cocked her head to indicate her surroundings. "I'm the proverbial old maid. I have seventy-nine cats to satisfy the stereotype. And you are?"

"I think what she was trying to say a minute ago was, she doesn't remember that detail."

Sam walked behind a chair and held it out. "Why don't you sit?"

His female charge nodded and sank into the offered seat. She crossed long, pale legs and Sam had to compel himself to drag his glance away. He took a chair between the two women, but was disheartened to see those attention-grabbing legs through the glass table-top.

What was with him today? You'd think he'd been marooned on a desert island for ten years with his *bada-bing-bada-boom* reaction to this woman. He'd been around female legs before, and they'd been around him. He cleared his throat at his unintentional risqué turn of phrase—and mind. He had a perfectly adequate girlfriend who had perfectly acceptable legs. *Get your mind in the game, Taylor, and off body parts.*

"You don't remember your name?" Beena gawked.

A small gray cat bounded into the mermaid's lap and she let out a gasp.

Sam chuckled at her goosey reaction. "There's a rule around here. No lap shall go unoccupied for more than—*oof!*" Gargantua, a twenty-pound calico, hit him in the gut. He gave the cat a jaundiced look as it settled on his thighs. "...Thirty seconds."

Sam's mermaid looked at the gray in her lap, then tentatively began to pat it. He watched her hand slide cautiously over the fur. He might not know much about her, but it was obvious she didn't have pets. She treated the cat as if it was a bomb that might go off any second. When she snagged Sam's gaze, he had the strangest feeling of being caught doing something wicked. "What's this one's name?" she asked.

"She's Gray Ghost," Beena said, turning to Sam. "She's on the list to be spayed. Bertha found her the last time she was on the mainland. The little sweetie-puss was really malnourished. But she's doing super now."

Sam reached over and patted the gray between the ears, being careful not to graze his mermaid's thigh. He didn't need her leaping up and screaming *pervert* in front of his aunt. ''I guess we'd better make friends now, little one,'' he said to the purring kitty, ''since you won't like me much for a few days.''

''Sam?'' Beena asked, ''did you order yourself some breakfast? And some for Angel here?''

''Angel?''

Sam peered at the young woman who'd asked the question.

''Yes, Angel.'' Beena smiled. ''You're Sam's Angelfish, aren't you?''

A frown formed between the young woman's brows and she passed Sam a look. Apparently she wasn't crazy about being called ''his'' anything. Considering she'd called him a pervert not ten minutes ago, he could see why she might be hesitant. He gave her a quick grin. ''It's as good a name as any until you remember yours. We have to call you something besides 'hey you.'''

She seemed to consider that. ''I suppose.''

Her lips lifted slightly, almost slyly.

Slyly?

Sam shook off the absurd notion.

"Angel it is, then," she said.

DANA HAD EITHER accidentally stumbled into an episode of the "X-Files" or she'd found a perfect hiding place. All she had to do was keep anybody who wasn't on the island from finding out she was there. That meant she had to make sure no communications about her were sent to the mainland, and the grinning pervert with the great pecs didn't go blabbing it around—wherever he was from.

Considering what she just heard, it sounded like this Dr. Sam Whatever would be staying on the island for at least a few days. Did she dare hope his stopover would last two weeks? How long did it take to doctor seventy-nine cats?

Seventy-nine?

Looking at Beena McQueen, Dana had to wonder about the woman's mental stability. With a purring cat collar and enough diamonds in that broach to pay Dana's librarian salary for the next decade, she wasn't your run-of-the-mill maiden aunt.

Completely sane or not, Beena's island was perfect for Dana's needs. All she had to do was make sure nobody radioed the coast guard or anybody else in Miami. Tate would monitor radio reports about somebody found paddling around in the sea. She was positive he wouldn't contact the authorities about her jumping ship. He'd want to quietly find her through his own sources, so there wouldn't be any bad press about her sudden change of heart. Tate was sure to count on his oily charm to change it back.

Not to mention her mother's whiny harangue. Dana cringed at the thought. Her mother had never gotten over the loss of the family fortune, though it had been twenty years. Dana's marriage to Tate had seemed like the perfect vehicle to replenish the family coffers, pairing the Vanovers's venerable old-money name with the Tates's nouveau wealth. Dana's mother's need to have her affluence and social position restored would blind her to any damning allegations Dana might have about Tate. She had no proof, just the fact that she'd overheard—

"Are you in pain?"

She jerked to stare at the doctor, noting his blue eyes had narrowed. His close inspection flustered her and heat rushed up her cheeks. She had the craziest notion he was trying to see into her mind. "Uh—no..."

"Did you remember something?"

She swallowed hard. "No—"

"Don't badger the poor thing, Sammy." Beena took off her glasses and let them dangle. The orange cat curled around her neck began to toy with the chain. Beena lifted a woven straw bowl and peeled back a linen cloth decorated with kittens. "Have a granola muffin, Angel, dear. I'm sure Cook is dispatching steamy coffee and other yummies to us this very minute."

Dana took a muffin, noting Beena's fingernails—long, each painted with a tiny image. She guessed they were cats. Every nail sported a different background color, and each finger held at least one gold ring encrusted with diamonds, opals, emeralds and all manner of costly gems. Dana was amazed the tiny woman could lift her hands. When Beena offered a knife and the butter dish, Dana pulled her gaze from the woman's hands.

"Thank you," she said, slathering butter on the muffin. To heck with cholesterol today. She'd almost drowned, so a little butter didn't look all that lethal. "Who does your nails?" she asked, trying to decide how to get to the subject of *Where's your VHF radio and how long is Dr. Blue Eyes planning to stay?*

"Madam Rex, my personal cat astrologist, does my nail portraits." She held up a hand, fingernails forward so Dana could better see. "Each is a work of art. Naturally I wear false nails, so after I've worn them, I can keep them in my fingernail portrait collection."

"She has over a thousand at last count."

Dana flicked her glance to Sam. His lips twitched, threatening to become a full-fledged grin.

"Oh, pish tosh!" His aunt waved him off as though he were so much flotsam. "Sammy is always kidding me about Madam Rex. He sees no purpose for either her astrological reading for my babies or the fingernail portraits." She gave her nephew a loving swat. "He's a perfect example of why I am single today. *Most* men have no sense of whimsy!"

Dana didn't know what to say, so she took a bite of the muffin. She wasn't sure she had enough whimsy to think cats needed their own astrologist. The fingernail collection was a little on the eccentric side, too.

"Ah, here's the fresh coffee and food," Beena said.

Dana glanced up to see two women, dressed in floral muumuus, hefting silver trays heaping with delicacies. After a flurry of activity, she found herself face-to-face with more food than she could eat in a week, starving or not. Nevertheless, she had a feeling if she'd been in an eating contest with a two-man team of ravenous truck drivers, she'd have whipped their tails.

Halfway through a heaping plate of hash browns, Dana came to the conclusion she would explode if she ate the forkful she'd lifted to her lips. Lowering it, she pushed the plate away with a sigh. ''Those were the best potatoes I've ever eaten.'' She reached for her napkin, but remembered a gray cat was sleeping on it. She wiped her hands on her shirt-front, giving the doctor a quick peek.

He lifted a brow as if to say, ''Gotcha!''

She pulled from his gaze and concentrated on the sleeping cat in her lap, stroking the soft fur between its ears. The act was somehow calming, a strange but pleasant encounter. Dana's mother was highly allergic to animals, so she'd never had pets. She smiled at the feline, thinking that since she had her own little house now, she might go to a shelter and pick out—

''How do you know?''

She shifted toward the doctor, confused. ''How do I know what?''

He leaned forward, resting his forearms on the table. With the move muscle flexed in his chest. "That those are the best potatoes you've ever eaten?"

The question jarred her. Had she actually said that? Good grief! Had the *gotcha* look meant he'd seen her use his shirt for a napkin, as she originally thought, or did he mean...

She sucked in a breath, staring first at him, then Beena, who watched her closely.

"Uh—" Her mind scrambled around for something to say, something plausible. "I—I guess it's not much of a compliment—since I can't remember anything. Huh?" She tried on a smile for size. It didn't fit quite right. "I—I guess we know one thing about me. I'm a cliché freak. I'll probably blurt out I'm 'busy as a beaver' or 'pleased as punch' or 'sharp as a tack' or..."

"'Lie like a rug'?" Beena said, looking delighted with the game.

"Yes, er, I mean, no. I mean—" She shut up. Babbling would only give her more chances to slip up.

When she peeked at the handsome doctor, she wasn't happy to notice that he continued to observe her. After a very uncomfortable moment, he pursed his lips. "Hmm-mm."

She felt even more uncomfortable after that long, drawn out utterance, dripping with doubt. How could she have been so stupid to say that about the dratted hash browns? Now he was suspicious. She could see it in his face. "What does 'hmm-mm' mean?"

"Nothing." He lifted a shoulder in a shrug and sat back. "Not a thing."

Yeah, sure! She went prickly with panic, but tried to remain outwardly calm. *Dana Vanover, don't go off half-cocked,* she admonished herself silently. "Hmm-mm" probably means absolutely nothing. He may say "hmm-mm" all the time—like some kind of stress-reducing mantra. Or he might have a nasal passage blockage, and that's how he clears it.

"I know!" Beena slammed her hands on the table, waking not only the gray cat in Dana's lap, but Gargantua and the orange fur collar. The sparkle of inspiration in the older woman's blue eyes didn't do a thing for Dana's heart rate.

"What do you know?" Sam asked, then winced as Gargantua rearranged her bulk in his lap. "Hell, cat." He looked down. "Watch the claws."

The calico yawned, stretched, and closed her eyes.

"Angel is a Cuban refugee!"

Dana was stunned. Whatever gave the woman such a nutty idea?

"Whatever gave you that idea?" Sam asked, and Dana experienced another prick of discomfort. He couldn't possibly read her mind, but his word choice was eerie. "Why would you think that, Aunt Beena? She hasn't spoken a word in Spanish."

Beena stroked the orange cat's tail and cackled. "Of course not, Sammy, love. She has amnesia. She can't remember how!"

Dana strangled a laugh, turning it into a cough.

"Yeah, well..." Sam passed Dana a look. "I bet Angelfish here would like to clean up and put on something besides my shirt. Wouldn't you?"

Dana nodded, figuring even an amnesia victim would know if she needed to wash her hair or not. "I'd appreciate it."

"Sammy, show her to the room next to yours. It's got a lovely view of the ocean." Beena picked up a silver pot and served herself another cup of coffee. "Do you have any clothes, Angel, dear?"

Dana was taken aback by the question and gave herself a heartbeat to make sure she would answer like a real amnesiac. "Uh, only what I have on."

"That's a lovely shirt, Angel." Beena took a sip from a fine china cup. Gilded figures of cats pranced nose to tail around the brim.

"It's my shirt," Sam said. "But thanks."

Beena smirked at him. "She looks well in your shirts. Why don't you let her have some of the clothes you've left here over the years? I'm too scrawny for her to wear mine, and I don't feel it would be right to impose on the help, do you?"

Sam frowned at his aunt. "So you impose on me?"

She set down her cup. "Certainly, Sammy. That's what relatives are for." She waved a hand. "Now off with you. Madam Rex and I have a full morning of readings." She reached over and poked Gargantua in her rump. "You're first, sweetie. Let's see what's in the stars for my voluptuous girl."

Gargantua peered at Beena and gave her an irritated-sounding meow.

"Sorry, old girl. I've got to go." Sam hefted Gargantua off his thighs and settled her on all fours. Immediately the cat plopped onto the shaded flagstone and began to lick her foreleg as though the move had been her idea.

Dana lifted Gray Ghost from her lap. It's little body was slack in her hands, as though it trusted Dana absolutely. She gingerly placed it on her chair and gave it one more pat before facing the doctor. "I—I don't want to be a bother."

"Not to worry, Angel, dear," Beena said. "Sam is such a clotheshorse, he'll never miss a few pairs of shorts and shirts. Sam?" She touched his hand. "I think that purple shirt with the big yellow flowers would do nicely, and the mauve and coral stripe. Oh, oh—that dazzling rose-colored one with the kittens all over it.'' She shook her head at him. ''Why you left those masterworks here, I'll never know.''

He bent to kiss her cheek. ''I must be insane.''

''Unquestionably, since they were all gifts from me.''

He winked in Dana's direction and she felt its affect sizzle in her belly. ''Clearly, I have a few bats cluttering up my belfry.'' He straightened. ''Are you still determined to walk on your own, Angelfish?''

She nodded. ''I'm much better, thanks.'' Now was her chance to find out how long he intended to stay. At the last second, she remembered her manners and turned. ''Thank you for the wonderful breakfast, Miss McQueen.''

''*Beena*, Angel, dear. Nobody calls me Miss McQueen.''

Dana nodded and smiled, then felt a hand at her elbow. "This way, Angelfish." He tugged her through the entrance they'd come out earlier. "We'll share a bath, but—"

"Like heck we will!" She jerked from his hold. "This may be a private island, but some social values still apply. I bathe alone, buster."

He glanced at her, his expression skeptical; a hint of mirth played around his lips. "You know..." He cleared his throat, as though he were swallowing a laugh. "The name angelfish suits you."

She frowned. "And since angelfish are pretty, I presume that remark is some kind of weird veterinarian come-on?"

"Angelfish are beautiful. However, I was referring to their attitude." He took her elbow again. "Angelfish can be cranky."

She glared at him. "Well, if I'm so offensive, why would you suggest we bathe togeth—"

"Let me clarify," he cut in. "We'll share a *bathroom*, but I'm clean, so you can have the place to yourself." He leaned toward her, eyes twinkling. "Does that arrangement abuse your social values?"

Dana swallowed hard. Humiliated, she shook her head. With a deep inhale of lavender-scented air, she prayed to be devoured by Gargantua—now!

"After you bathe, feel free to rummage in my closet." He spoke matter-of-factly, and Dana was grateful for small favors. At least he'd resisted the impulse to call *her* a pervert. "I'd appreciate it if you'd pick from the pastels," he said. "No matter how much Beena enjoys buying them for me, I don't look good in pink and lilac."

She chanced a peek at him and his troubling grin. She hated the way that crooked show of teeth made her breath leave her body. *Dana, get your mind on what you're supposed to be doing!* she warned herself. *Don't let a set of straight teeth and a well-developed tanned male body, sidetrack you. Focus!* "What are you going to do?" She gritted her teeth, wishing the question hadn't come out sounding so desperate. She wanted to seem casual.

He tugged her around a bend in the candlelit hallway. "I'm going to get my medical things off the boat."

The boat! He had a VHF radio on the boat! Agitated, she chewed the inside of her cheek. "Are you...are you going to call the coast guard about me?"

"Why?" He indicated stone steps curving upward and out of sight. "Is there some reason I shouldn't?"

She swallowed around a lump of panic. "No—I mean—why should there be?"

He continued to hold her elbow as they started up the steps. She wondered if he was being gallant or if he wanted to guarantee she didn't make a break for it. After seeing Beena's ostentatiously displayed wealth, Dana could understand why her nephew would be distrustful of strangers who appeared on the island—no matter how innocent their arrival might be.

She stopped abruptly. "No!"

Sam glanced at her. "No? Are you saying you don't want me to radio the coast guard?"

She manufactured a laugh, as gay as she could muster. ''Not that. I just realized how selfish I've been. First making you carry me up here, with me snapping at you all the way. Now you're forced to turn over your clothes!'' She shook her head. ''No! I wouldn't think of bathing and relaxing until I've helped you carry up your things.''

''That won't—''

She threw up a halting hand. ''Ah! Not another word.'' She about-faced so quickly, she almost tumbled down the stairs. Sam's quick reaction saved her when he slipped an arm around her waist.

''Whoa,'' he said. ''There's no big rush.''

She warily removed herself from his touch, but some irritating imp in her brain made note of how warm and firm he felt. ''Uh...but there's no reason to put it off, either.''

''You're not up to carrying stuff up from the boat.''

''Pish tosh.'' She mimicked Beena with another laugh. ''Sammy, lead the way!'' He could be right. She was awfully wobbly, but she hid her exhaustion. This was important!

Her attempt at levity didn't make him smile. As a matter of fact, it inspired a wrinkling of his brow. He scrutinized her for several ponderous ticks of the clock, and she had the same scary feeling he was trying to get inside her mind.

He looked as though he was about to object once and for all. She knew she'd better show him she was adamant. Now! "I refuse to bathe until you say yes." She crossed her arms in front of her, attempting to look as unmovable as a giant redwood.

His expression grew wry. "There's that charming pit bull quality again."

She experienced a prickle of irritation. "This time I know you're calling me a dog!"

"Not technically." He took a step down. Moving ahead, he startled her when he took her hand. "If nobody's reported you missing," he muttered, "We'll know why."

She eyed him furtively, but made no comment.

When her father passed away the year before—rest his sweet soul—Dana lost her protector, her champion. She sorely missed the anchor of trust and wisdom he'd been in her life. If she had any chance to shatter Tate's scheme, she had to stay hidden, and had to figure out a way to accomplish that—alone. Therefore, there could be no communicating to the mainland about amnesiac blondes being fished out of the sea.

When she noticed Sam watching her, she gave him her wide-eyed, one-celled-organisms-outscore-me-on-IQ-tests look. *You'll never know if I've been reported, Doc,* she threw out telepathically, daring him to read her mind.

Dana's dad had been handy with tools. Being Ray Vanover's daughter, Dana knew how to repair a VHF radio. It would be a piece of cake to sabotage one.

CHAPTER THREE

DANA TAGGED A STEP BEHIND her doctor captor, his hand clasping hers as he led her down the gradual sloping landscape. They exited the grounds of the castle and set out across sandy dunes and seagrass toward the cabin cruiser.

Dana didn't know much about boats, though she'd lived in Miami all her life. Her mother hated the water, so even before her father lost his fortune in several ill-timed ventures, they'd never owned a boat. But Dana's father, being the great guy he was, had always been willing to help friends who needed something fixed on theirs—be it the radio, the engine, fog lights. He could fix anything. And so could Dana, since her dad let his adoring daughter tag along.

Her legs quivered as she shuffled over the uneven ground, but she mastered her fatigue and set her mind on the problem at hand. ''So, how long did you say you'd be staying on the island?''

He glanced her way. "I don't think I said."

She stumbled over a clump of seagrass and fell to one knee. Thank goodness he didn't release her hand or she wouldn't have had the strength to stand.

"Are you sure you're up to this?" he asked.

She smiled as brightly as she could, but even her face muscles were pooped. "I'm as tack as a sharp! I mean—*sharp* as a *tack*."

His brows went up in blatant skepticism. "You really are into clichés, aren't you?"

Dana decided it would be better to speak in clichés to keep herself from saying anything too distinctive that might give away the fact she was faking amnesia. She shrugged. "I never promised you a rose garden, Doc."

His lips quirked. "And old song titles."

"Is that a song title?"

He shook his head. "Never mind."

He pulled her along. As she tramped through powdery sand, she grew more and more irritated that he hadn't answered her question. She decided to try another tack. "How long does it take to doctor seventy-nine cats?"

"Depends on their condition and needs."

She made a face at the back of his head. He was being so darned evasive you'd think she was asking for top secret military codes or something. "Okay, then how long, in general? Usually?"

He glanced her way. "In general, usually, it depends on their condition and needs."

She fought the urge to kick him in the shin. "Oh?" She tried to look amused. "That long?"

They reached the dock. The creak of boards under his deck shoes and her bare feet were the only sounds, except for the piercing cry of seagulls and shushing water swirling around the pilings.

Sam let go of her to climb into the boat. She had half a mind to leap into the water and find another island without any veterinarians hanging around all buff and tan and skeptical, wearing nothing but shorts and shoes. Facing the fact that she was being silly, Dana climbed into the boat after him. Even if she had the strength to swim more than fifty yards, this place was perfect—sexy, irksome veterinarian or no sexy-irksome veterinarian.

Once on board, Dana glanced around, guessing the cruiser was about forty or forty-five feet long, not new but in good condition. The doctor clearly was a shipshape kinda guy. She glanced forward to scan the helm, and spotted the VHF radio.

''I'll go below and get the supplies,'' he said, drawing her gaze.

Experiencing a surge of relief, she nodded. Good, he wasn't going to call the coast guard immediately. ''Wild horses couldn't drag me away. I'll hold the fort and I won't move a muscle.''

His brows dipped with her newest plunge into Cliché Bog, but he didn't comment. She smiled innocently. *Just stay below long enough for me to zap your VHF.*

He disappeared down the steps. She tiptoed to the helm, hoping the boat didn't creak and give away her sneakiness. Swiftly, she reached behind the radio and located the screw-on coupler, easily removing it and disconnecting the antenna. The next time Sam keyed the mike to send a message, he would blow the radio into VHF heaven. Since the sabotaged radio would die without a whimper, he would have no idea why it didn't work.

Her heart pounding with guilt, she tiptoed back to where she'd been standing. Not a moment too soon, either. The pesky pet doctor stomped up the steps, hefting an armload of boxes. "Take what you can. I'll carry the rest."

She grabbed the top two. "What's in these?"

"Medical supplies."

"No kidding?" She tried to mask her exasperation. "I was sure you were a gun runner, arming the cats for a revolution."

He'd bent to set the other boxes on deck, but peered at her. "Why don't you take those on up? Eartha will show you the clinic. Wait for me, there, and I'll show you to your room—and the bath.''

A blush crept up her neck at the reminder of her bathroom blooper. He emphasized that last part on purpose, the bum! Deciding she needed some breathing space—and enough distance to keep from strangling him—she gave a saucy nod. ''Aye, cap'n.''

When she reached the ladder, she couldn't figure out how to get down and hold on to the boxes at the same time. After a minute of uncertainty, she felt the containers being lifted from her hands. ''Climb down. I'll hand them to you.''

''Good idea.'' She avoided eye contact, unsure what exactly was causing her bashfulness—the zapped-radio guilt thing or the buff-tan-turn-on thing.

Safely on the dock, she had to look up into those troubling blue eyes. She noticed how thick his lashes were. Bedroom eyes! That's what the doc had. The kind of eyes that sucked you in and made you feel all melty, and want to tear off clothes—his first, then yours. It was

a good thing he was a dog doctor, since any
bedside manner that included those eyes would
cause female patients to rip out stitches trying
to jump his bones.

''Hey, earth to Angelfish,'' he said. The ap-
pearance of brown cardboard in front of her
eyes snatched her back to reality. She grabbed
the boxes and angled away. ''Catch you later.''
*And good luck contacting the coast guard, Doc
Bedroom Eyes.* She was glad her back was to
him. Any suspicions he had about her would
only intensify if he saw her smirk.

Now to find the radio in the castle—and
fast.

EARTHA LED DANA to an interior room very
different from the rest of the castle. It had a
white tile floor and walls, and looked like a
doctor's office, which it clearly was. One area
was partitioned off for surgery. Eartha showed
Dana where to store the supplies, then left her
there to wait for Sam.

As soon as the security chief was gone,
Dana scurried into the hallway, checking

rooms swiftly, stealthily, hoping to find the communications center in this lavender-scented maze. When Sam found out he couldn't call from his boat, he'd head straight for the castle's radio. She figured she had ten minutes, max.

She chewed the inside of her cheek. ''Now, if I were a radio, where would I be?''

She heard a sound and flattened herself against the wall, grateful for the dimness. Eartha appeared in a doorway, then headed down the hall, away from Dana. After Eartha disappeared around a corner, Dana darted to the door, peaking inside.

There it was! The radio. A floor unit, it was an unassuming boxy setup with glowing indicator lamps and a microphone for transmitting. But it wasn't a VHF; it was a satellite system. That made sense, since VHF radios had limited range. But it was okay. She could handle it.

As she tiptoed in, she quickly surveyed the room, noting there was also a console and several monitors, showing various views of the island's coastline. This must the security head-quarters as well as the communications center.

Dana didn't know where Eartha had gone, but figured she'd be away for at least five minutes. That's all she needed. Now, if only her luck would hold, and Eartha's brawny twin didn't suddenly appear and kick unattractive dents in her head.

Hurrying to the radio, Dana gave it a quick once-over to find out where the coaxial cable feed line led from the radio. As would be expected, it skirted along the wallboard, then at the corner, snaked up the wall to disappear through the ceiling, no doubt winding its way to a satellite dish positioned someplace on the vast roof.

She slipped off one cubic zirconia earring, grateful they'd survived the trip with her. The earring clutched in her hand, she squeezed her upper torso behind the radio to reach the wall-board.

Thrusting hard, she stabbed the cable with an earring post, then snapped off the fake di-amond head. The broken metallic piece, buried inside the cable, would short circuit the signals. Though her sabotage wouldn't damage the transmitter or receiver, the radio was off the air until she—or somebody else—removed the metal post.

No matter how desperate she was, Dana couldn't leave a whole island full of people helpless in case of a life-threatening emergency. She could only hope that Eartha was hired more as a leg-breaker than an electrician. Luckily for Dana, even a good electrician would need pretty advanced technology to detect the tiny metallic fragment imbedded in the cable. From the look of it, Beena's equipment was not cutting-edge technology.

Silently she eased out of the tight space and beat it back to the doc's headquarters.

The scrape of shoes brought her up short as she realized Sam was there ahead of her. *Drat!* What was she going to tell him she'd been doing?

"Doc?" she called.

"I'm over here."

He was behind the partition.

Stealthily, she stuck the cubic zirconia inside her bra to dispose of later, then she arranged her face to look harmless and not quite bright. She didn't want him thinking she had the mental wherewithal to vandalize anything that required the cunning of a two-year-old. "Oh? I was just over there." She forced a giggle. "How did we miss each other?"

He didn't respond. She tried not to let that fact bother her, and strolled around the partition. "So, this is where you fix broken kitties?"

He removed bottles from a box and began to place them in a shelf over a white countertop. She figured the bottles were antiseptics and other specifics needed for surgery, but opted not to ask, since he'd probably just say they were bottles.

When he emptied the box, he turned and shot her a critical squint. Though the look lasted only a fraction of a second, it jarred her. Without a word, he walked to the wall and pressed a button. "This is Sam. I'll need the operating room scrubbed down before tomorrow morning.''

''I'll see to it, Doc,'' came the squawky response. ''Glad to have you back.''

''Thanks, Mona. It's good to be back.''

He released the intercom button and headed toward Dana. When he gripped her elbow she winced, anticipating a harsh grab and a demand to know what she'd done to his radio. The harsh grab she braced for turned out to be nothing more than a light, guiding touch. There was no shouted accusation, either. She peeked at Sam's face, checking for signs of irritation, or even an indication that he was aware his radio had met with foul play.

He smiled benignly. ''Now, Angelfish, I'll show you to your room.''

It took her a few steps to get herself together mentally. ''Uh...who's Mona?'' She hoped she sounded conversational.

''She's Aunt Beena's personal secretary and animal psychic.''

Dana was more than a little startled that he'd given her a straight answer. Or was it? ''Animal psychic?''

He ran a hand through his hair but didn't glance her way. "Right."

"Your aunt has a cat astrologist and an animal psychic?"

"Mona prefers Trans-species Clairvoyant Dialogue Expediter."

Dana couldn't help giggling. "I'll try to remember that."

"Or you could call her Mona."

She smiled. "You're very indulgent of your aunt and her eccentricities. That's sweet."

"I owe her a lot." He looked at her, then turned away. "And I love her."

Dana felt a renewed stab of guilt. He seemed basically nice. But as the old saying went— *the nut doesn't fall far from the insane family tree*. Besides, he had his own little quirk of feeling up strange women who washed up on beaches.

She glanced at his somber profile and had another thought. Maybe he really was trying to be helpful. She didn't want to soften toward him. He was so cute, liking him might be risky. After the Tate debacle, she didn't intend to get involved with any other men until they'd proved themselves six ways to Sunday. She made a face. Was that a cliché? Whatever, she wasn't into "trust" these days, especially with people who might not be rowing with all their oars.

She decided to get her mind back to the subject at hand. "How long has Mona-the-trans-species-clairvoyant-dialogue-expediter-personal-secretary been here?"

"The house is ten years old. That long."

Dana glanced around as they entered a large room. The walls were stone, the floorboards polished, and the windows strongly defined. Cats lounged or scurried around in the cool, dimly lit room. Tall wrought iron candle holders, encrusted with melted wax, held flickering beeswax candles that gave the place a mellow glow.

Sam didn't say any more as he pulled her along. At the far end of the hall, he led her up a set of wooden steps into a narrow corridor. A few steps ahead, she recognized the curving staircase they'd only made it halfway up earlier.

"So where did Beena live before ten years ago?"

"Miami." Sam tugged her up the stairs. "My aunt had fifteen cats then, which was over city ordinance maximum. She decided to get a place where she could set her own limits."

Dana laughed. "She certainly did that. Couldn't she have bought property outside the city and been able to keep her cats?"

Sam glanced at her, his lips quirking. "From what you've seen so far, does my aunt impress you as someone who would do what most people would do?"

Dana shrugged. "Now that you mention it..."

His brow creased. "You've lost an earring."

Dana almost reached up, but caught herself. "Earring?" She kept her face blank. "I—I didn't know I had any on."

He touched her naked earlobe. "I was sure you had them both earlier."

She made a show of feeling the ear after he'd lowered his hand. "Really?" She touched the other earring, pretending not to be familiar with it. "What does it look like?"

"A little square diamond."

"A diamond?"

"I'm a vet, not a jeweler. Since you've lost one, I hope it's not real."

"Me, too." She bit her lip, deciding that's what someone with amnesia would do if she thought she'd lost a real diamond. "What a shame."

"Maybe we'll find it."

Not if I have anything to do with it, Doc! She smiled wanly. "I'll hold a good thought."

They reached the top of the stone steps and Sam indicated a long hallway, not surprisingly hung with more tapestries. "Mine is the first room here. Next is the bathroom." He stopped in front of a third door. "This is yours, but you'll have to go into mine to get the clothes."

He pressed a wrought-iron handle and the door creaked open.

"Make yourself at home," he said, and she realized he was leaving.

"Where are you going?" she asked, hoping he hadn't detected anxiety in her voice. What difference did it make, now? She didn't need to watch him like a hawk any longer. He couldn't call anybody, and he wasn't going far. She knew he would be here for several days. She smiled lamely. "I mean—what should I do when I'm—I've changed?"

He pressed the door wider so she could see the deep, arched windows. Bright sunshine spilled inside, illuminating a room sparsely furnished with strong, unadorned furniture. "Just look out the window." His offhand wink did weird things to her insides. Before she found wits enough to respond, he was gone.

DANA FELT a thousand times better after her shower. One thing about Beena's medieval castle, was the totally modern luxury of the bath. The spacious chamber held a huge

Jacuzzi tub and a separate shower with two shower heads that belted out the nicest, most relaxing spray. She could have stayed there all day.

The only stupid thing she'd done, no doubt due to being extremely tired, was forget to find any clothes before her shower. So now she stood in front of Sam's closet wearing nothing but a towel. It didn't make for a leisurely perusal. She kept worrying that he'd burst through the door. Of course, the towel covered a lot more of her than her underwear had, so she didn't know why she was worried. He'd already seen—and felt—more of her than... She swallowed hard. Well, more of her than any veterinarian had a right to. She gritted her teeth and redoubled her determination to get this over with and get out of his room.

She yanked out several hangers containing pastel-colored shirts. But what about shorts? With a pile of pastels over one arm, she scanned his room, wondering where he kept his pink pants.

His room was much like hers, but his bed was bigger and didn't have heavy woven hangings draped over it. Hers had a canopy of bright pink and purple tapestry that matched the spread. Sam's bedspread was woven with more earthy colors. Darker and more masculine. The floor was covered with the same woven rushes. Around the room and between his tall, arched windows were chests, coffers and straight chairs of simple plank construction. In one corner resided a table consisting of a wide board resting on trestles. As well, there were a few bronze art pieces and hand-thrown pottery jugs and bowls scattered about. Once again, Dana felt as though she'd been swept back in time. Amazing.

Enough gaping! She had *shorts* to find. She couldn't spend two weeks wearing nothing but men's shirts. She decided to check out the tall wardrobe opposite the bed. Inside she found drawers of underwear, socks and *finally* shorts. There were a couple of pairs of yellow linen shorts, several in emasculating shades of violet and rose, and even two pairs of madras walking shorts. She smirked. She hardly knew Sam Taylor, but since most of these pants sported store tags, she sensed he wouldn't mind if she confiscated them.

''Now for underwear,'' she muttered.

''There are some silk boxer shorts over here.''

She spun around, her heart jamming in her throat. Why didn't his door creak like hers did!

He closed the door with a soft click, his expression wry. ''Sorry. I figured you'd be finished by now.'' He ambled to a tall chest and pulled out several silky items. She stood dead still, shirts and shorts crushed to her chest. She only hoped her towel didn't come lose because of her violent wheeling about.

He eyed her speculatively. ''Okay, I'll come to you.'' He held out the short stack of boxers. ''This is the best I can do underwear-wise. Sorry.''

She managed to free up a finger and stretched it out. He hooked the elastic of all five pairs around it, and she clamped the finger back. ''Thanks.'' Darn, she could feel her towel giving way! With both elbows she held it firmly at her sides, but she knew her backside was out there catching the breeze. Thank goodness the bathroom was on the same wall as the wardrobe. She started edging sideways. ''I'll...I'll just go get dressed.''

''You do that.'' He watched her, looking baffled by her sideways withdrawal.

His quizzical expression became too much for her and she halted. ''My towel's coming loose!'' she said. ''That's why I'm walking this way.''

He didn't quite grin, but his eyes made a mockery of his serious expression. ''Angelfish, I hate to be the one to break this to you, but you're standing in front of a mirror.''

She gasped, spun around, then sensed her horrible blunder and whirled to face him again. Mortified and flustered, she half tripped, half stumbled backward into the wall. Pressing her naked derriere against rough, cool plaster, she glared at him. ''You think this is *funny?*''

He peered at her from beneath craggy brows. His hand covered his mouth. With a brisk shake of his head, he turned away. ''Nope.'' He cleared his throat. ''Not at all.'' He coughed. She knew he was trying—and failing—to hide his laughter.

''Pervert!''

''For owning a mirror?''

''You could have warned me!''

''I thought that's what I did, Angel.''

How dare he be logical at a time like this! *''Ooo-ooh!''* She lunged toward the bathroom door.

''I've decided to shower. Let me know when you're through in there.''

''Listen up, Doc, and you'll know!''

It took two seconds for Dana to reach the other side of the bath and dash into her room. She slammed the door with all the strength her humiliation could produce, then reached for the lock. To her dismay, there wasn't one. ''Oh, fine!'' Spinning away, she inspected the room for something heavy she could shove in front of the door. Not that she believed Doctor Laughing Hyena would barge in. She just didn't like knowing that a man who was suspicious of her, an expert with sharp instruments—and seriously warped—had the *choice*.

She chose a trunk with rope handles, and dragged it over, shoving it against the door with a loud thud.

"What the hell are you doing?" he asked from the other side of the door.

Dana cringed and sank down onto the trunk. She didn't know what was inside it, but dragging it from the foot of the bed had used up the last of her energy. "Nothing," she wheezed. "Don't mind me."

"You're barricading your door?"

She squeezed her eyes tight. He was too perceptive. "Apparently you've heard the sound before," she said, too tired to do more than loll her head against the wood.

She didn't hear a sound for a full minute.

"By the way, Angel, the VHF radio on my boat doesn't work."

She sucked in a shuddery breath and counted to ten before she tried her voice. "Oh?"

"Neither does the one in the house."

"Really?" Her heartbeat thundered, but she forced herself to sound confused. "What... what does that mean?"

"Why don't you guess?"

"I'm, uh, not very good at guessing games."

"How do you know that, Angel?"

She covered her face with her hands and cursed herself, wishing she would learn to keep her mouth shut. "I mean—I'm too tired to think straight. I don't understand." She yawned. That was no lie. She was dead on her feet "What are you saying?"

"I'm saying, we can't contact anybody."

"Not even the coast guard?"

"Right," he growled. She heard water and realized he'd turned on the shower. "Not even the coast guard."

CHAPTER FOUR

DANA WOKE and winced with pain. Coming up on one elbow, she realized she was lying on the floor in a position that would indicate she'd slid off the trunk she'd jammed against the bathroom door, and sprawled on her face.

She shook her head to clear her sleep-fuzzy brain. She'd slept like a corpse. "I'm surprised there's no chalk line around me," she muttered.

She could tell from the dim light, it must be nearly nine o'clock in the evening. She'd been asleep for more than twelve hours.

Struggling to her feet, she grasped the towel around her and moved to the window. Long, long ago, Doctor Burst-in-the-Room had told her to look out the window when she finished her bath. He probably hadn't meant fourteen hours after her bath, but it was the path of least resistance and she didn't feel like doing much heavy-duty thinking right now. She was wobbly, woozy, and starving.

Scooting onto the deep window ledge, she clutched the towel to her breast and peered outside. Lanterns burned around the perimeter of the patio and the pool. Reflected firelight sparkled in the fountain and waterfall, but what snagged Dana's immediate attention was the annoyingly robust doctor, swimming in the pool. Apparently he was doing laps, because when he reached one end he executed a quick, racing flip and headed back the other way.

Dana was a strong swimmer, but she was impressed by the doc's seemingly effortless style. Slumping against the wall, she watched him eat up the distance, then flip and reverse direction.

''Enough!'' she told herself, hopping down. ''Get dressed. Didn't you learn anything from Tate? There's more to determining the worth of a man than great pecs and a tight tush.''

Tate was a handsome, smooth devil who'd swept Dana off her feet. On her next dip into the finding-a-man waters, she planned to pick some shy twirp who spent his leisure time in library stacks humming sickly sweet ballads, researching the habitat of the dung beetle, and respectfully referring to her as ma'am.

She walked to the bed where she'd tossed the armload of men's clothes, and was startled to see a cat curled in the middle of them. "Well—" She eyed the creature skeptically. "I don't remember seeing you on any hangers in the doc's closet."

The feline, a rather random concoction of black and white blotches, lifted its head and yawned.

"How did you get in here?"

The cat didn't look interested in responding. It took a leisurely lick of a paw then resumed its nap.

Dana glanced at the closed door. In the fading light she noticed the pet door. Amazed at herself for her lack of alertness, she ran both hands through her hair. She must have been more exhausted than she'd realized. Facing the kitty, she gently extracted a flowered shirt and a pair of yellow shorts from beneath it. "Forgive me, your majesty,'' she said. ''I'll be out of your way in a minute.''

The cat stirred, seemed to frown, then began to snore.

Dana slipped on the shorts. They left a bit to be desired in the ''perfect fit'' department, gaping at the waist. She looked as if she'd been half devoured by a yellow shark.

She dragged the wooden chest away from the bathroom door and went in to retrieve her bra, dry by now. Heat warmed her cheeks when she realized the doc couldn't have missed her flimsy lingerie hanging there on the same rack with the hand towels.

She hurriedly slid it on, then the shirt. Barefoot, she padded into the doc's room to look for a belt. Since he was swimming, she knew he wouldn't burst in on her. Besides, she was dressed, so that doubled the odds he wouldn't show up.

She couldn't find a belt, but spotted a rack of silk ties. Most were pink or magenta or rose, so she had a feeling they weren't at the top of the doctor's I-must-wear-these-immediately list. She picked a coral and chartreuse paisley and ran it through her belt loops. Cinching it, she headed out of his bedroom and down the stairs. With only one or two wrong turns, she finally found the exit to the patio.

"Greetings and salutations!"

Dana recognized Beena's squawky welcome and looked around, spotting her sitting cross-legged on the patio, near the fountain. Two cats sat in her lap. The orange kitty still hung around her neck. Another woman sat beside her. This one—a gaunt cadaverous creature with long black hair—looked up. Or at least Dana had the feeling she did, though she couldn't detect any movement.

Beena's fingers sparkled as firelight reflected in her jewelry. "Come here, Angel, dear. Meet Mona. We were just completing our Trans-species clairvoyant dialogues for the day."

Dana managed a smile, adjusting her features to look minimally bright. Pretending to be a blonde dimwit in front of the skeptical doctor was her safest route, and would probably go unnoticed by his eccentric aunt. She waved. "Why, hello, Beena."

"Sit!" Beena motioned toward the flagstone. "Mona, this is the sweet little package I was telling you about. Sam fished her out of the sea." Beena gestured as Dana took a seat on stone still warm from the setting sun.

Dana noticed Beena's knees, knobby and sunburned, jutting out of baggy denim shorts. Red and yellow argyle socks fought for color palette supremacy over turquoise-and-plum beaded moccasins.

On the other hand, Mona's palette contained only one color. Black. From her straight hair to her lipstick to her monklike garb, she resembled a big, dormant bat.

One other element to Mona's attire drew Dana's gaze, unsettling her. Hanging from the breast of her smock were small reptilian-looking brooches. *Yuck!* Dana thought. *Of all the jewelry choices in the world! Tiny Tyrannosauruses!*

"How do you do." Mona-the-bat stuck out an emaciated hand.

Her long, curling nails were shiny and black. With more trepidation than Dana had ever felt just shaking hands, she reached toward the woman. As their fingers touched, Dana felt a blow, and screamed. An embarrassing second later, she realized she wasn't suffering some horrible bat-woman touch of death. A chubby kitty had pounced into her lap.

She covered her thudding heart with her hands. "Oh—I'm *so* sorry! I—I'm not used to…" She wanted to say, *Shaking hands with the living dead* but opted for "…cats jumping into my lap. It scared me."

"So your memory has returned."

Dana jumped in alarm. The doctor sounded way too close to be swimming laps. She looked around. He stood a couple of feet behind her. His quizzical expression aimed her way, he began toweling off. The dripping swimsuit clung to him in all the right places, hinting at things better left unhinted at. She pulled her glance away. It slid down powerful legs, then, rethinking, shot above his waist.

The muscular contours of his torso caught the flickering firelight just right. Drat! No matter where she looked, there was something to be avoided.

Irked at herself, both for her aroused turn of mind and yet *another* slip of the tongue, she spun away. "How could I possibly be used to having cats jump in my lap. I have amnesia," she rejoined.

So there!

"Stop teasing the poor dear, Sammy, love." Beena beckoned. "Come join us." She turned to Dana. "I imagine you're starving, Angel."

Dana couldn't deny it, and nodded. "I don't mean to be a bother, but I am hungry."

"I'll tell Cook," Mona said in a low-moan-of-cold-wind monotone. For a cadaver, she moved swiftly. Her vacated place was immediately filled with cat. It was almost as though the animal just lay there as the ghost-bat-woman's molecules scattered and reassembled around it.

When Mona turned her back, Dana notice with alarm that one of those ghastly pieces of jewelry was crawling up to perch on her shoulder. She heard a scream and realized it had come from her own throat.

Mona didn't react, but Beena touched her knee. "What's the matter, dear? Did Parsley claw you?"

Dana peeped askance at Beena. "That dinosaur brooch *moved!*"

"Oh, that." Beena tittered. "They're not brooches. They're baby iguanas. Mona has a number of them as pets. She hangs the babies from her clothes. That's how they bond."

Bond? Dana found that vaguely disturbing. "I—I thought they were jewelry."

"Oh, Mona doesn't believe in jewelry," Beena said with a gay cackle. "She's a rabid back-to-the-earth person."

Dana didn't doubt it. Rabid-bat-woman looked as if she'd be perfectly at home *under* six feet of it.

A scraping sound drew Dana's attention. Against her better judgment she turned to see the very-nearly-naked doc pull up a metal chair. He turned it around to face away from them. Straddling the seat, he settled down and rested his forearms on the chair back. "Have a nice nap, Angel?"

She shrugged. "I fell asleep on a trunk, slid off and ended up taking a siesta on the rug."

His grin was crooked and bothersome. "That explains the waffle pattern on your face."

Unable to squelch a blush, she self-consciously touched her cheek, praying it was dark enough so her flush wouldn't be detectable.

"Maybe I should have explained about beds and what they're used for."

She gave him a narrow look. "No, thank you. I'll just struggle along in my ignorance."

"That's a good sign!" Beena clapped her hands.

Confused, Dana turned her way.

"How is that a good sign, Aunt Beena?" Sam asked, once again echoing Dana's thoughts.

"She said *siesta!* Don't you see? Her Spanish is coming back."

"It's a miracle," Sam said.

Dana glanced his way, noting his taunting grin, his eyes glittering with mirrored flame.

"Pretty soon she'll regain her memory and we won't be able to understand a word she says!" Beena went on, clearly not grasping her grand-nephew's sarcasm.

"You haven't asked about the radios."

Dana felt a stab of misgiving, but masked it with wide-eyed dumb innocence. "Radios? What radios?"

"Remember, I told you the VHF on my boat and the satellite system don't work?"

"Oh? Must have slipped my mind." She gave him her most innocent severely-mechanically-challenged look. "I guess we'll just have to watch TV."

Beena giggled. "Not that kind of radio, dear. Our communication radios. We can't call anybody."

Dana screwed up her face to look bewildered. "Don't you have a phone?"

"No, dear," Beena said through a sigh. "We have to use radios from way out here in the boonies.'' She scratched her orange kitty between the ears. ''Isn't it the strangest coincidence that both our radios would go out on the same day?''

''Very strange,'' Sam said.

Dana forced herself not to look at him, worried that he might see something amiss in her eyes.

''We can't imagine what's wrong.'' Beena shook her downy head. ''Luckily, the mail and supply boat comes in a week. We'll get a message to the mainland about needing repairs.''

Dana's heart lurched to her throat. She shifted to face Sam. ''A week?'' *This was bad news!*

He nodded. ''You don't have any urgent plans, do you?''

Yes, and they don't include a boat showing up in one dratted week! ''I—how would *I* know?''

He gave her a long, scrutinizing look—head to toe, then toe to head. She grew restive under his inspection. What did he think he was looking for that required so much investigation? "Checking for fleas, Doc?"

His lips quirked. "How do the clothes fit?"

Dana hadn't expected such an abrupt subject change. She wanted to grill him about the supply boat. But she decided she'd better not rush things, or appear too agitated. With a shrug she hoped looked breezy, she said, "Loose, but comfortable."

"You look very whimsical, dear," Beena said, plainly unfazed by the zigs and zags of topics. "Sam is such an unwhimsical dresser. I try to whimsy-up his wardrobe, but he resists."

Too aware of the doctor's mellow laughter, Dana looked at the furry beast curled on her legs. She noticed with some surprise she was petting it. She also noticed she was too aware that Sam's leg was practically brushing her arm. He must have dried off from his swim, because she could swear she felt radiant heat from his calf. She set her teeth, irritated with herself. She didn't need to be thinking about his heat!

In the silence, she heard a noise and wondered which cat growled, then registered with chagrin that the noise came from her stomach.

"I'll check on that food," Sam said.

As he stood, his leg brushed her shoulder. She gave him a look that was half grudging, half grateful and half fearful. Or was that too may halves? Whatever, she felt all three emotions. She had a feeling he received all three. His wink was impertinent and disabling. He was ambling away before her breathing kicked in. She stared after him, grudgingly inspecting the flex and bunch of muscle—doing exactly what muscle was meant to do in extremely well-toned male bodies.

"He's a nice boy, my Sammy," Beena said, drawing Dana's attention. "Don't you think he's a nice boy, Angel?"

She cleared a rustiness from her throat. "Oh, I—yes, I'm sure he's…nice."

Beena chortled. "For somebody without a speck of whimsy, you mean!"

"Not a speck," she admitted.

Dana ripped her gaze from the doc's brawny back. *He might be short on whimsy,* she grumbled inwardly, *...but for a man who didn't trust her as far as he could throw his boat, he sure was obscenely long on whoop-de-do!*

LOGICALLY, SAM KNEW the woman sitting on the patio, playing bingo with Beena, Mona, Madam Rex and Bertha, couldn't possibly have sabotaged the radios. Even from his vantage point above them, from the window of his room, he noticed it had taken several rounds for the blonde to figure out that she was supposed to look *down* the column, beneath the letter that had been called out, to see if the matching number was on her card. She gave every impression that somewhere out there a village was missing its idiot.

On the other hand, his Angelfish might be the shrewdest little vixen he'd ever run across. Just what her game was, he couldn't imagine. But he knew it had something to do with swindling his great aunt out of her money. He'd had experience with innocent-looking types before who'd wangled their way into Beena's off-center world. His aunt was too trusting. She'd been robbed before, and he damn well didn't intend to let it happen again.

Sam had tried to put a stop to it by personally doing all Beena's hiring. The past five years had gone fairly smoothly for his great-aunt and her comical little queendom—*not* one hundred percent, though. And that one mistake rode Sam hard.

There was something about this leggy blonde that troubled him. Something *besides* her long, pale legs and her wide, green eyes. Ever since she'd washed up on the island things had seemed strangely out of kilter.

He planted the flat of his hands on the deep windowsill and examined her with a critical squint. She said something and laughed. The others joined in. She didn't give off treacherous vibes; she just seemed friendly and not quite bright. His emotions warred—was she that innocent, or that shrewd?

He frowned, angry with her. No, damn it! He was angry with himself. He found her annoyingly tempting, and that made him nuts. He had a girlfriend! He'd been content with Liza for four years. And here came this woman, crawling out of the sea....

He bit off a curse. Two radios blowing on the same day, practically at the same time, was so bizarre he had trouble believing it was a fluke. Angel had been alone—in the proximity of both—moments before they were discovered to be malfunctioning. He eyed her narrowly, his gaze drifting without permission to her legs as she recrossed them beneath the glass tabletop. She had the legs of a swimmer, or a runner, well-toned yet feminine. But she was so pale, unusual for Miami residents in mid-June. Of course, if she were a con artist from out of state, a strong swimmer with an electrical engineering degree, that would explain a lot.

Sam was no engineer, so he had no clue how a nearly naked woman, without access to even a screwdriver, could disable the radios, and in only a matter of seconds. In all likelihood she was as innocent and dumb as she looked.

Just in case, though, he planned to keep an eye on her—day and night.

DANA HAD NEVER SPENT such a weird, intensely exhausting day in her life. She'd been awakened at seven o'clock when a breakfast tray was delivered to her. She was told by the maid to report to Doc Sam's "surgery" by seven-thirty, and to change into the hospital scrubs waiting for her in the office.

Dana hadn't been happy about it, but "Doc Sam" turned out to be the kind of man who didn't take no for an answer. He'd been waiting, already dressed in greens. He'd explained that his assistant, who usually came with him, was seven months pregnant and her husband hadn't wanted her to leave. So he needed Dana's help. *Period.*

Without a say in the matter, Dana reluctantly learned what Sam called the "Spock Death Grip" for holding cats immobile while being given shots. She'd unwillingly become accomplished in administering ear mite medication, but hardly adroit at avoiding getting the stuff all over her and in her hair when the cat tried to shake every last molecule out of its ears. She'd learned that cats can and do—without the slightest hint of regret or remorse—spit pills at the unsuspecting pill-giver, and that most cats resist being flea-dipped with every fiber of their being, not to mention claws and teeth.

Dana was positive her skin had absorbed enough dip to keep her protected against flea infestation for the next ten years.

Oh, and one other thing. She'd learned that it's politically incorrect to toss one's cookies directly on the cat—or on the doctor's shoes, no matter how gross the medical procedure.

These were revolting, wearisome lessons Dana hoped she had no reason to remember, but she had a gut feeling she'd better try.

She looked around the office and spotted the wall clock. Nearly six. She stretched to get the kinks out of her spine. For the past hour she'd been updating medical files while the doc checked his patients, now resting in cages.

Some cats, which had received less intrusive treatments, were released on their own recognizance. Others roamed the office, awaiting the doctor's say-so before they could regain their freedom. A tortoiseshell cat with an angelic face and rotten personality, plopped down in the middle of Dana's paperwork, apparently believing batting at her pen was just the right cure for its head cold.

Dana gave it a severe look. "You're slobbering purple baby aspirin juice on my records, cat."

The feline rubbed Dana's knuckles with the side of its face, leaving a glob of purple slobber.

"Yuck!" Dana wiped her hand on her soiled greens.

"The torti's marking you as her property," Sam said. "Which is generous, considering she hates taking pills, and anybody who dares to try to feed them to her."

"No kidding?" Dana held up her bandaged thumb. "I thought she just enjoyed a hemoglobin chaser after a session of spitting pills in my eye.'' Her right eye still stung and watered from that fiasco.

Dana could tell when Sam came near. The hair at her nape stood up. She was so provoked with him for what he'd forced on her today, she itched to get her hands on his neck and squeeze until he coughed up a fur ball. Unfortunately, she didn't have the strength.

Besides being drained physically, she was worn out emotionally. She'd never been so frightened or upset in her life as she was this morning when he'd demanded that she assist him in the clinic. After all, there were at least fifty other people he could have shanghaied to help him. But no! He'd ordered *her* to do it.

She had been horrified. She knew nothing about animals! She'd never even had a pet, but she couldn't tell him that and still stick to her amnesia story. So, without argument, she'd kept her irritation and fear to herself and done her best. It had been hard to hold on to the dumb blonde act, too, since she didn't want to kill any kitties by pretending not to understand his instructions. All in all, it had been a rotten day.

Dana avoided looking up at him, though one watery eye was hardly working, anyway. Instead she concentrated on the cat and its single-minded batting of her ballpoint. She couldn't help visualizing the doc in her mind, the way he'd looked today. Even though most of the time he'd worn a surgical cap and mask, she'd had to struggle with the melting effect his azure bedroom eyes had on her. Those thick, dark lashes slanted her way whenever he'd ask for a sponge or suture or swab.

Once, she'd been positive he was laughing behind that mask. Okay, so she probably looked hilarious when she was up-chucking, but he could've had the decency to show the tiniest shred of concern.

"Are you hungry?" he asked.

Startled by his question, she wasn't sure her shrug looked all that casual. "Well—lunch didn't stay down long."

His laughter was rich and deep. Her skin grew warm at the sound. "You did fine."

When he rested a hand on her shoulder, she went rigid.

"Dinner should be ready in about thirty minutes. Go on up and shower."

The torti batted at Dana's pen, knocking it from her debilitated fingers. "Uh, what about these files?"

"They'll wait."

"And—the cats?" She couldn't imagine why her voice was so faulty, or why she wasn't dashing pell-mell out of the room.

"The night shift's coming on. I'll stay to leave instructions. When you're out of the shower, knock on my door."

She nodded, clearing her throat, thinking *Get your hand off my shoulder so my stupid body can move!* It nearly shocked her out of her seat when he did as she'd mentally commanded. A shuffling sound told her he'd turned away. "Thanks for the help, Angelfish."

She shifted to frown at him. "Thanks for the *help?*" There was no mistaking the derision in her tone. ''Are you suggesting I had a choice?''

He opened the cage door for Gray Ghost and began to stroke her furry back. When he glanced at Dana, his grin was as annoying as heck. ''Go shower.''

He turned away and spoke softly to the little gray. Dana continued to scowl at him with her good eye. Just then the purple-dribbling kitty took it upon itself to rub slobber against Dana's jaw, leaving a dank trail. She twisted back and made a face. ''Give me a break, Catastrophe, or whatever your name is!'' She swiped at the goo. ''You nearly put out my eye earlier. Isn't that enough abuse for one day?''

''Something wrong with your eye?''

She was *really* sorry he'd heard that. She'd tried to keep the teary side of her face away from him. ''No, not a thing. I'm as healthy as a horse.''

''Let me see.''

She pushed up from the chair, giving the torti a darn-you look. ''I'll be going now.''

She shuffled sideways in her attempt to escape, but his hand at her elbow dragged her to a halt. "I'd better check that eye. The cornea might be scratched."

"It's not. It's fine."

"Don't you want a doctor's opinion?"

"Not especially."

She felt his fingers on her jaw, urging her to face him. "Don't make me use the grip, Angel."

She was beginning to see that Doc Sam got exactly what he wanted, exactly when he wanted it. Bully that he was. Since he outweighed her by at least fifty pounds, she decided she had no choice but to give him his way. She didn't have to be happy about it, though. She lifted her chin and glared one-eyed at him. The other eye watered and teared. "Look, I'd be thrilled for your professional opinion if I needed worming," she said. "But in case you hadn't noticed, I have human eyes!"

"I noticed."

With her one good eye, she met his two very exceptional ones. He squinted slightly. "Hold still." He leaned closer.

She tilted backward until she was bowed over the desk like a reading lamp.

"Darlin', if you lean any farther you'll be lying on that desk and I'll be on top of you. Is that *really* the position you want to be in while I examine your eye?"

Some evil imp in her brain applauded and hooted with glee at the prospect, but Dana's better judgment grabbed hold of the idiot imp and shook the stuffing out of it. She clamped the desk edge with her fingers. "Just hurry."

With a gentle touch, he held her eye wide, dipping closer, closer. A flicker of panic chased through her, and her breathing became shallow. She swallowed, but her throat was dry.

His breath warmed her cheek. She could detect his scent, clean, manly, with a hint of antiseptic. It wasn't a bad smell, just unusual. Like his eyes.

She watched those eyes as he examined her teary one. "It's not scratched," he said at last.

When his gaze met hers, the effect snatched her breath away. She blinked, and lowered her gaze. "Thanks. I—I told you...." *Why didn't he back off?*

"When you take your shower, flood it with warm water."

She nodded. "Right—warm *waaaaaaaaaaaaouch!*" Something jabbed her in the backside. She jerked forward, slamming into Sam. Reflexively, she grabbed his neck. "Something stabbed me! Or bit me!"

"What the—"

His arms came around her.

"Am I bleeding?"

"Do you want me to check?"

"*No!*" she cried, realizing where he'd have to look. "That cat attacked me!"

His chuckle rumbled through her. "Pouncer. Bad girl."

Frowning, Dana peered over her shoulder. The torti's head was down, ears back, butt up and tail swishing from side to side.

"Don't even think about it, Pounce!" Sam's tone was a little too amused for Dana's taste.

She sucked in a shocked breath when his hands slid to cup her bottom. "What do you think you're doing?"

"Covering the target."

"Yeah—well, that's not what it feels like!"

He released one cheek and slid open a desk drawer. Dana watched as he tossed something to the opposite side of the desk. "Okay, Pouncer, get the tuna munchie."

The cat's ears shot up and her butt went down. An instant later she'd pounced on the kitty treat, no longer interested in Dana's posterior.

"Pouncer likes you," Sam said as his hand returned to cup the unprotected cheek.

Dana shifted to meet eyes, which sparkled with unrepentant laughter. "Pouncer needs therapy," she muttered. "Doesn't your aunt have a cat psychologist on the premises?"

"She's vacationing in the south of France at the moment." He scanned her face. "You know what, Angelfish? I've discovered a couple of important facts about you, today.''

She experienced a jolt of trepidation. *Drat!* She'd tried so hard to keep her wits about her, even when she was barfing. How had she slipped up? ''What—important facts?''

''You're not a doctor.''

Relief made her weak and she scowled at him. ''Did the upchucking help with that deduction?''

His grin flashed, bright and appealing. ''It didn't hurt.''

She made herself frown. ''And the other thing?''

''You're not a mother.''

That insight took her by surprise. She wasn't, of course, but how on earth would he know? ''Don't tell me you can detect an episiotomy scar through a woman's clothing?''

His eyebrows lifted a fraction. ''I'm good, but not that good,'' he said. ''No, it was when you tried to stick that rectal thermometer in Gray Ghost's mouth.''

"A mother would know better than that, huh?"

He nodded, but only faintly. His eyes remained on her. *Those dratted, beautiful, taunting eyes.*

Dana found his closeness and his intimate touch way too stirring. All she needed was to rebound into this good-looking doctor's arms. *No!* She'd learned her lesson where it came to smooth, sexy studs. She would never again be swept off her feet by good pectoral muscles and the whiff of agreeable pheromones. The next man she got involved with would *prove* his worth, *show* he was honorable, trustworthy, and most importantly of all, willingly grovel at her feet. Dana had a feeling the doc didn't grovel well.

Steeling herself, she fought her attraction. "There's an important fact I've learned about you, too." The assertion came out breathy.

His long lashes slid to half mast, a cruelly erotic act. "Really?"

"Mm-hum."

"What fact?"

"The fact, that if you don't get your hands off my posterior, you're going to be walking funny."

His brow furrowed slightly, but an instant later he grinned and stepped away. "Thanks for the   insight."

"My pleasure, Doc." Avoiding further eye contact, she slid from behind the desk and skittered out the door.

CHAPTER FIVE

SAM WATCHED HER LEAVE his office. Sometime after she was gone, he noticed he was still standing there, grinning at the empty door like some infatuated doofus. He glanced at his hands, oddly cupped, as though her tush was still...

He made a disgusted sound and dropped into the seat behind his desk. Pouncer had curled herself in the middle of his records and was watching him intently, purring. He eyed the cat with skepticism. "Did you have any idea what you were doing, young lady?"

She extended a forepaw and lay it atop his hand, then rested her head on the outstretched foreleg. Her purring continued unabated.

Sam grinned wryly and shook his head. "I can see you feel real bad about it."

Pouncer closed her eyes, seemingly content in the knowledge that she held him captive beneath her paw. A dribble of purple slobber escaped from the side of her mouth and oozed onto a hapless medical record.

"She's not as dumb as she pretends."

Pouncer opened one eye.

"There aren't many people who can learn to shave a cat for surgery that quickly. Besides, if she were as dumb as she wants us to believe, she wouldn't know an episiotomy scar from an Iggy Pop video."

Pouncer leaked another purple globule of drool.

Sam bent down as though confiding a secret. "She isn't being straight with us, Pounce. That can't be good."

The feline closed the eye, purring and drooling.

Sam straightened, watching the exit through which his blond enigma had recently departed.

He had no proof she was lying about anything. Just because she'd caught on to what he needed her to do in the clinic didn't mean she was a calculating sleaze hiding behind a mask of big-eyed dumbness. Maybe she simply had a knack for nursing animals—that is, after she got past the puking.

What was her game? Or was she even playing? He'd never felt so torn in his life. He'd watched her closely all day. She'd been distracted and upset and even sick, yet she hadn't said a word that suggested she didn't actually have amnesia. Still, there was something elusive about her that disturbed him. Something he couldn't put his finger on.

He heard a noise and realized two staffers with first aid training were coming to take over the night shift.

Enough woolgathering! He was a doctor, and his work wasn't done. He patted the cat and stood. ''Don't shove her into me again, Pounce,'' he murmured. ''It's a bad idea to get hot for a con artist—no matter how nicely her derriere fits into my hands.''

AFTER A LATE DINNER Beena, along with her quaint sorority of oddballs, shambled off to bed. That was an hour ago. Dana was tired, but too restless to sleep. It hadn't dawned on her until a short time ago that this was Saturday night.

Her wedding night.

She experienced a twinge of sadness for what might have been—if Tate had been the man she'd believed him to be. In all her twenty-six years, she'd never fallen so hard or so fast for a man. He'd played her like a pro, pressing all the right buttons, and she'd taken his handsomely displayed bait like a starving guppy.

She supposed his yacht had been an echo of the glittery life-style she could only distantly recall, and she'd been sucked in. Dana hated herself for her unforeseen streak of shallowness. But she supposed she couldn't have lived with her mother all those years and not have some of that ache for The Good Life rub off.

Dana slid her hand along the stone banister as she trailed slowly down the steps that led from the upper patio to poolside.

She flicked away a tear. "Don't you dare feel sorry for yourself, nitwit!"

Listless, she leaned against the railing and stared up at the sky. The night was full of stars—millions and millions of them, so radiant, innocently twinkling, giving off all that beauty for free. She felt a pang, unhappy to realize the idea of anything being given away free seemed foreign to her now. Her experience with Tate certainly had taught her a scary lesson about life and people.

She inhaled, the soft scent of tropical flowers filling her lungs. Another benevolent gift. A fresh tear trickled down her cheek as she stared at the stars, wishing she had no reason to be startled by the beauty of nature and how it was so unselfishly and freely bestowed on the world.

The flickering torches cast everything in a russet glow. The pool, with its underwater lighting, seemed blinding compared to its surroundings. She turned away, deciding she needed darkness. She wandered onto the lawn, heading nowhere in particular. Dana never had a wedding night before. She wasn't sure how one was expected to spend it—alone and feeling violated.

The kitties that had romped everywhere only an hour ago were nowhere to be found. Dana had a feeling several of them would be snoozing on her bed when she went inside. Funny, the idea of finding small, furry beings on her bedspread didn't bother her nearly as much as it would have a few days ago. She'd learned a lot about cats today—and more than she cared to know about their doctor. Like the fact that he had long, expressive hands, nimble, gentle fingers, and an endearing tenderness in his voice and his eyes as he soothed and calmed panicky animals.

When he looked at her, that tenderness became shadowed with caution. He *sensed* she was lying. She knew he'd decided to keep an eye on her, no doubt to make sure she wasn't casing the joint for vaults to pilfer. Things would be so much easier if he weren't so darn perceptive. Maybe a veterinarian had to have keen insight, dealing with patients who couldn't communicate by words.

She'd been so careful, trying not to give him any more ammunition for his suspicions. Had something in her posture or her expression added to his misgivings, or was she reading wariness in his gaze simply because her ability to trust had been crippled?

Her wedding night. She inhaled to staunch another surge of self-pity.

Just as she had been duped into falling for Tate's suave line, her mother had been beguiled by his promise of a money-making property that would return her family to the pinnacle of Miami society. Something her mother had craved for the past twenty years. *How perfect,* both she and her mother had thought. Dana did, after all, love Tate Fleck. How marvelous to match his flair for enterprise with their proud family name.

Only by accident had Dana thwarted Tate's plan, overhearing him drunkenly jeer to an accomplice how the money-making property was a dead loss, rife with labor dissent and a harbor for his lowlife buddies.

She had also discovered, to her shock and anguish, that Tate's big business deal was completely bogus. He'd needed a venerable old name—which her family's reputation could provide—to run a scam that would net him a fast fortune before the bottom dropped out, ruining thousands of small investors. By then, however, Tate would have disappeared, leaving Dana and her mother, Magda, to cope with the scandalous aftermath.

Dana wondered what Tate was doing right now. Had he been interviewed by the media, fielding question about where his bride had disappeared to? Had he made up some excuse—that she was ill?—determined to find her before it was too late for him to pull off his fraud?

And what about her mother? Dana knew Magda Vanover well. Blinded by the need for status and wealth, Magda would remain staunchly at Tate's side, parroting anything he told her to say. Mrs. Vanover would assume Dana had caught a case of cold feet, and would be retrieved, reassured, and then walk submissively into holy wedlock with Tate.

Holy! That was a laugh. ''Unholy'' was more the word for what that lying, cheating slimebag planned. Tate was a determined, ruthless man with powerful allies. Dana didn't know who she could trust, didn't dare confide in anybody. Her only hope was to stay hidden until the clock ran out on his scheme.

That deadline was still nearly two weeks away. As long as the deal simmered, Tate would rip apart heaven and earth to find her. He would make their wedding a reality, even if he had to use force.

She couldn't let that happen.

''No way!'' she vowed grimly.

''There's always a way, Angel,'' came a disembodied voice. ''What is it you want?''

Dana spun, stunned at how close Sam sounded. She pressed her hands to her thudding heart. ''Are you trying to scare me to death?''

His husky laugh filled the night. ''If I'd have wanted that, I'd have jumped out at you and said *boo.*''

She caught movement as he stepped out from behind a clump of palmettos.

Though the night was black, the torches touched him with sufficient light to show off wide shoulders and a nicely contoured chest. He wore dark, baggy shorts, yet enough of his long, athletic legs were visible to be bothersome.

"Do you do a lot of creeping around barefoot in the bushes, or have you decided to become my personal stalker?"

"Your personal stalker." His grin was a sexy flash. "If you'd give me a hint about where you're going it would make stalking you at night much easier."

"Why didn't you say so, Doc?" She shot him a sarcastic grin. "I *live* to make your life easier."

His easy chuckle made her suddenly nervous. Not scared nervous. Female nervous. Drat the doctor! He radiated a wily charisma that reached out and nudged her libido. *No!* she told herself. *No more good-looking, sexy-grinning, masterful hunks for me. No more making value judgments with my eyes and my hormones! The next man who turns me on will do it with sparkling conversation and a willingness to ask my permission to kiss my feet!*

Besides, the doc didn't trust her. He was out here spying on her to make sure she wasn't absconding with the family jewels.

She made a point of turning away. ''I'm just walking.''

''A night person, huh?''

Oh, no, you don't! You won't make me slip up that easily! ''I have no idea.''

''Why don't I walk with you?''

''That's not necessary.''

''I think it is.''

She faced him. ''Don't you trust me?''

He winked. ''Come on.'' He took her arm and began to steer her across the lawn. ''There's a path not far away that leads to the beach.''

She didn't pull from his grasp, and that made her furious with herself. The last thing she needed was to go all tingly about a man who was only there to make sure she didn't commit any Class-A felonies. "I gather you're a night person?" she asked, trying to sound one notch above bored.

"Depends on the night."

She didn't respond. Something about his answer was too suggestive to even go there.

They headed down an easy grade toward the wall that separated the velvety lawn from the sand and dune grass. The stone structure looked to be about five feet high. When she halted, so did he. "How do we get over that?"

"I'll lift you."

She peered at him. "Some great pathway to the beach."

He grinned. "Don't worry. It's there."

He tugged her along. When they reached the stone barrier, he let go of her arm and stepped behind her. "When I lift, you swing up a leg and get a hold."

"Really? I thought I'd go limp and you could toss me over."

He laughed and took hold of her waist. His hands felt warm and strong against her bare skin. Suddenly, Dana regretted tying the tail of his shirt beneath her breast. She didn't need his hands on her at that moment. Heck, she didn't need them on her at all!

"On the count of three."

"What?"

"Jump on three."

"Oh, now I've got to *jump,* too," she scoffed. "What exactly are you good for?"

He released her. "Okay. You jump. I'll watch."

She eyed him with animosity, then braced her hands on top of the wall. She'd show him she didn't need or want his hands on her! With a mighty push, she swung a leg up. Before her trembling arms gave way, she'd levered her upper torso high enough to drop, stomach first, onto the stone surface. She cringed at the slap she got, and feared she'd scraped her belly, but refused to groan.

She took a couple of breaths and used her remaining strength to right herself. Once she'd settled on top of the wall, her feet hanging over the far side, she smirked at him. "Piece of cake."

His grin crooked, he nodded. "Congratulations." He placed the flat of his hands on top of the wall. With a mighty leap, he cleared it, landing with hardly a sound on the sand. The jump across took all of a second. Looking as though hurdling tall barriers was no more exerting than stepping over cracks, he leaned against the wall a hairsbreadth from her leg. "Do you want help down, Tarzan?"

She surveyed the terrain. The slope here was steeper. If she missed her step, she could end up rolling a long distance—possibly spraining and breaking bits and pieces of herself along the way. She faced him without enthusiasm. Tall, with the deliciously fit body of a pro baseball player, he watched her. Dana watched him back, cursing herself for not being able to pull her gaze from the display of corded muscle, flexing and coiling, in the dimness.

After a strained minute he held out a hand in silent invitation. The move shook her out of her daze and she jumped down, determining that broken body parts was a chance she had to take.

She made a perfect two-point landing, then in an alarming turn of events, slammed to the flat of her back. The wind rushed out of her in a painful *whoosh*. She lay there, wide-eyed. Stars darted and tumbled around in the heavens. She squeezed her eyes shut. *Drat!* They were still shooting and zipping and somersaulting! This wasn't a good sign—not to mention the fact that she couldn't breathe. She gasped and winced, gasped and winced. Finally, glorious air began to trickle into her lungs.

"Yes, I can see that was a much better plan."

A fire burned in her chest and he was making jokes! Opening one eye, she glared at him, but she was still too occupied with taking in air to tell him to go to blazes. Even so, she held up a hand and shook a finger at him.

He knelt and grasped her wrist as though he were taking her pulse. "It's a little fast."

She opened her mouth, but could do nothing but gasp for air.

He settled on the sand, facing her. Releasing her wrist, he leaned across her, resting his hand in the sand near her waist. Their hips touched, but any erotic stirrings were overpowered by her desire to live.

He watched her solemnly for a moment. Then his lips began to twitch. *"¿Habla Español?"*

"No—" she wheezed. "I didn't—get my memory back, if that's what you're groping for." She glowered. "I think—my back is broken, in case you're interested."

A dark brow rose. "Oh?" He lifted his hand from the sand and trailed a finger across her bare belly. "Feel that?"

Her mouth opened in shock. She certainly did! To be agonizingly honest, she felt *that* in parts of her body that weren't even close to the skin above her navel, but were, evidently, hot-wired directly to it. This irksome winking-smirking-touching vet knew more about the female anatomy than he could possibly have learned in vet school.

He returned his hand to her side, but this time his arm made contact with her waist. "Well?" He cocked his head in question. "Feel anything?"

"Okay. Okay," she muttered. "I guess it's not broken." She pushed up to sit, and brushed his arm away. "I seriously doubt that your stomach-finger-brushing thing is a recognized test for loss of sensation, though."

"It's real new." He offered her a hand. "I realize this is futile, but..."

She was shaky, and told herself she was tired from clambering over the wall. With great reluctance, she accepted his hand. "Just pull."

He straightened to stand, hefting her up. She felt wobbly and flinched at the stab of pain coming from her tailbone. She was sure to have a bruise tomorrow.

He didn't let go of her hand, tugging her down the slope. "I love the ocean at night."

She peeked at him. He was a step ahead of her, pulling her along the path. The moon was a sliver of weak light off in space, but she could see well enough. The sand was so white it fairly glowed with a strange luminescence.

The night breeze tossed her hair and caressed her scorching face. Her stomach sizzled, and she had a sinking feeling it wasn't due to the scrape, but the remnants of the doc's absurdly erotic touch.

If she were to tell the whole truth, it wasn't pain she felt, it was the stirring of banked fires. This was her wedding night, after all. She'd been preparing for tonight with every fiber of her being—the fulfillment of her love for a man who'd turned out to be a world-class stinker. Dana supposed it wasn't all that odd that she might react strongly to another good-looking man who touched her intimately and gave off sparks of sexuality. She was primed, and he was prime.

She compelled her gaze away from his broad back. She didn't need this! What was she doing out here with him, anyway? How did this hap— Oh, *right*. He was suspicious and didn't plan to let her out of his sight.

She glowered at him. "My spy submarine is a thousand yards out. How am I supposed to signal it if *you're* hanging around?"

He turned and winked, and her stupid knees went mushy. "That's the point, Angelfish."

She yanked from his grasp. "You *really* think I'm up to no good, don't you?"

He gave her a level look, his smile dimming. "It's crossed my mind."

She wished she could tell him the truth. But she didn't know what he might do. He seemed honest enough, but so had Tate. Just because this guy was good to animals didn't mean he couldn't be bought.

She cast her gaze to the sand, staring absently as the ocean pushed a frothy offering almost to her toes, then with a whispering sigh returned to the sea. "Well, I'm not." With a rush of bravado, she looked him straight in the eye. "I'm exactly what you see. Nothing more." Okay, so that was a lie. Two weeks from now, maybe she'd tell him everything. But not now.

He pursed his lips, those bedroom eyes lazily taking her in from her breeze-tossed hair to her flip-flop rubber sandals, compliments of Cook. When his gaze returned to her face, he grinned. "Ever been skinny-dipping, Angelfish?"

"Uh—" Thank heaven she was so stunned by the question it took her a few seconds to respond. She had just enough time to remember she wasn't supposed to know if she'd ever been skinny-dipping or not. "I—I sincerely doubt it!"

"Wanna go?" He reached for his waistband, plainly intent on shoving down his shorts.

"*No!*" She whirled away. "Don't you dare take off your clothes!"

"Too late." She heard a slap-splashing sound. He was running into the surf. "Are you sure you don't want to join me?"

She gulped in a breath, which wasn't easy for some reason. Her heart thudded a mile a minute. "You're a pervert, you know!"

"The water's great."

"You're twisted!"

He didn't answer.

"Did you hear me?" she called. "You're sick!"

No response.

Finally, she had to turn and look. What if he drowned out there? "Sam!" she called. "Don't be a fool! You're not supposed to swim alone—especially at night!" She bit her lip. Would an amnesia victim know that? Darn the man and his trickery. He did that on purpose to fluster her and make her flub her story. He hadn't been able to do it all day while he'd sliced and stitched and lanced revolting pustules. How crafty of him to get her to blunder just shucking his swim trunks.

"Sam!" she cried, fighting an unwelcome stab of worry. He was nowhere to be seen. *"Sam!"* She jabbed a finger down at his swim trunks, her glance following. "Come back and put on these..." Where were they? She let the command trail off. There were no swim trunks on the beach!

He'd been *teasing* her! "Why you..." Planting her fists on her hips, she shouted, "I hope you *drown!*" Twirling away, she trudged up the sandy beach toward the castle. "It would serve you right!"

When she looked up, she stumbled to a halt. There in front of her, lounging casually on the wall, was Sam, glistening and grinning. He sat up and made a "come on" motion.

With clamped jaws, she marched forward.

"Miss me?" he asked, brushing wet hair off his forehead.

She scowled at him, then shook her head. "What are you, some kind of spook?" His grin was so irresistible and utterly unfair she wanted to smack his knee. "Shouldn't you be checking your patients or something?"

"Just did."

"Maybe you should check them again."

"Your concern is admirable." He jumped down with easy grace and relaxed against the wall. "Does this mean I'll see you bright and early in the clinic?" He crossed his legs at the ankles, idling there, tall and handsome. *The rat.*

"Do I have a choice?" she asked, startled by the raspy quality of her voice.

"No choice at all, Angelfish." He grinned.

She opened her mouth to protest, but anything she might have been about to say flew out of her head when he took her into his arms and hoisted her to the top of the wall.

She squealed, then gasped as her bottom was settled onto cool stone. Before her head quit reeling, Sam catapulted himself to the other side. Dana felt his hands at her waist, and all too quickly her feet touched grass. He let her go, and she sagged against the wall.

"That wasn't so horrible, was it?" Amusement rode his tone.

She ran a hand through her hair and glared at him. "You had no right to do that!"

"I thought I was helping."

She was angry, both at herself for her ridiculous heart rate, and at him for taking such physical liberties. Was there no escape from dominating men? "Well, you weren't helping.

You were *controlling!*'' She pushed away from the wall. ''I resent your suspicions, Doc. Don't believe for one second I don't know why you're keeping me practically glued to your hip in that clinic! But I'll do it—I'll do it because I owe your aunt for her kindness, and because I know how much she loves her cats. But I want you to be assured, if it weren't for her, I wouldn't set foot in that clinic! I *hate* controlling men, and never again will I allow a man to maneuver me or coerce me into doing anything! Is that clear?''

She stalked by him, aware that his grin was gone. *Good enough!* she thought.

''So, we have a past, do we?''

CHAPTER SIX

"SO, WE HAVE A PAST, do we?" Sam's question echoed in Dana's brain, firing a shot of terror through her. *Oh, no!* She'd revealed too much! With an apprehensive inhale, she spun on him.

His gaze was speculative under drawn brows.

What was she going to do? Her mind stumbled around for something credible. Anything. Any thread to clutch. She lifted her chin as she stalled and struggled for a believable insight. *"Maybe!"* she blurted, fighting to gather her wits. "Maybe—maybe your man-handling brought something to the surface."

There! That was good! She could go with that! She chose her words carefully. "I don't know what exactly it was. But, yes. Yes, obviously I've known men like you in my past, and it seems the experience was vastly unpleasant!" She regarded him with searching

139

gravity. Was he buying this? "I should thank you for bringing back a sliver of my memory—no matter how distasteful you were going about it!" Dana couldn't imagine why she felt it necessary to make such a cutting remark. Or possibly she knew. She needed to make sure he didn't smile that sexy smile at her again.

He pursed his lips, looking annoyed, then, after a tense moment, he shrugged. "Glad to be of service, Angelfish." Dana was startled when he took her elbow. "Allow me to *control* you back to your room."

She glared at him, and tried to pull away, but failed.

His response was a calculating grin. "Maybe on the way, I can provoke a few more memories."

"I don't see why not! You're the *most* provoking man I've ever met!"

"To your knowledge, you mean."

She glowered at him. "I'm willing to give you the benefit of the doubt."

His chuckle was hardly more than a grunt, and Dana sensed it held little humor. "Your dumb act is blown, Angelfish."

She peered his way. "Uh—what dumb act?"

"The one where you look at me with those big green eyes and pretend you don't understand the meaning of the word 'salad fork.'"

She harrumphed. "That's two words." They arrived at the patio steps, and Dana felt as if she was being dragged to the gallows. He was right, of course. She'd completely forgotten her naive-blond guise tonight. "Why would anybody *pretend* to be dumb?" she asked, hoping she sounded sincere. "You're as nutty as a fruitcake—as crazy as a loon—bigger than a bread—uh..." She ran a hand through her hair, thinking fast. She was scraping the bottom of her cliché barrel.

"It's not going to work this time," he cut in.

Feeling trapped, she glared at him, but opted not to respond.

He opened the door that led in from the patio, allowing her to precede him. "You're smarter than you want us to believe. What are you hiding?"

Though he'd let her go as she entered, once inside, his hand closed around her wrist. It was quite dim, with a few dwindling candles to light their way. A sleeping cat, here and there, stirred or meowed at the audacious interlopers. Dana clamped her jaws. She had no intention of making any admissions.

''Well?'' Sam coaxed.

She didn't face him, though he'd dropped back to be even with her. ''You're a suspicious man. I'm sorry for you.''

A tense minute passed as they began to climb the stairs. She could feel his stare. ''Is that all you have to say?''

''No.'' She pulled on his grasp. ''You're hurting me.'' She shifted to glare at him.

His jaw muscles clenched. ''No, I'm not.''

She yanked. ''It's my arm and I say you are!''

''Quit yanking and it won't hurt.''

She halted, forcing him to come to a stop. Halfway up the curving stairway, candlelight from the top of the landing faintly touched them. Dana leaned against the wall and raised her captured hand in front of her face. His touch wasn't painful. Not physically, but she didn't relish her tingly reaction.

''What are you up to?'' he asked. ''Don't tell me you're a karate expert, and you're getting me in position to throw me down the stairs.''

She shook her head.

''What, then?''

It almost made her smile to realize he not only doubted her, he was a little intimidated by her. Or at least what he imagined she was capable of.

She grinned in spite of herself. No man on earth had ever been intimidated by Dana Vanover. Though she was capable in a lot of areas—she fixed cars, did her own taxes, even replaced roof shingles—no man on earth had ever been *intimidated* by her.

Because she idolized her father, she'd always held men in some awe. Luckily, she hadn't fallen head-over-heels in love before smooth-talking Tate came along, or she might be a babbling idiot in some home for terminal suckers by now. Well, Dana was a fast study. She wouldn't make *that* mistake, again. Her father had been the exception in men, not the rule.

So here she stood, connected to this big, strong hunk, and he was intimidated by the mystery she presented. No doubt Sam envisioned her as some kind of Emma Peele character or female James Bond of the underworld. How laughably irresistible!

"What are you smiling about?"

She shook her head and stifled the grin. "Nothing. Just—never mind..." Unfortunately she wasn't in a position to share the joke with him. Dropping her arm, she resumed her trek up the stairs. Sam remained a step behind her, and it almost seemed as though she pulled him along.

Maybe Sam was a man she could get to grovel, after all. He was a gorgeous man who believed she was a crook. From time to time, didn't all men fantasize about walking on the wild side? Was she "the wild side" to the kitty doctor?

They reached the top of the staircase in silence. The thick stub of a beeswax candle flickered atop a tall, iron stand. The faint sweet wax fragrance mingled with the lavender permeating every castle byway.

Dana faced him, far from surprised that he observed her grimly. She smiled again, her mystery-maiden flight of fancy providing her with a curious boldness. ''Thanks for the escort, Doc.'' With a tug, she indicated her desire to be released. ''I'd invite you in for a drink—'' she fluttered her lashes, mischievously ''—but, I don't like you.''

He watched her closely without releasing her arm. ''What's going on, Angel?''

He clearly sensed her change, but didn't know what to make of it. She lifted a shoulder in a subtly flirtatious shrug. In all honesty, she had no idea what she was doing. She only knew it was fun being enigmatic for a change. ''Why, whatever do you mean, Sam?'' She gave the query a decidedly coy tone.

Sam's lips parted slightly. His puzzlement tickled Dana. She had never toyed with a man.

Never even flirted. Her new brazenness was due, in part, to Tate's harsh lesson. But she was also reacting to the fact that this should have been her wedding night, and that this powerful male animal, with the bedroom eyes and silky touch, turned her on unmercifully. To think he might willingly become putty in her walk-on-the-wild-side hands, titillated her.

She was a bubbling cauldron of mixed emotions—angry at him for what he'd put her through in the clinic today, and for his everlasting suspicions. But unhappily for Dana, her body throbbed with a wayward urge to taste his excessively kissable-looking lips.

You are a sick woman, Dana Vanover, she warned herself. But she was a woman *first.* A woman, who for the first time in her life, deliberately and with malice of forethought, wielded power over a man—even if her only true power was the tired old fantasy of tasting forbidden fruit.

"You want to kiss me, don't you, Sam?" she whispered, astonished to hear such nervy words coming out of her mouth.

His eyes widened slightly and she reveled in her power. Her sly smile fairly screamed, *I am forbidden fruit. Lust after me!*

He hesitated, measuring her quizzically. Dana could tell he was no longer in full command of his world. This moment of indecision was doubtless the first twinge of uncertainty in his adult life. *Good!* Let him be insecure. See how he liked it, for a change!

''Yes,'' he said, sounding hoarse. ''I guess—I do...''

Warming to the experiment, she lifted her chin.

She watched as he swallowed, plainly tossing around the pros and cons. Should he or shouldn't he? She was a stranger who had washed up on his beach, practically naked. Her arrival was mysterious, and very likely a foreboding of treachery afoot. It was a romantic scenario suitable to open any James Bond movie.

She wanted to laugh out loud. Dana Vanover, treacherous librarian of mystery!

Something hot and sizzly touched her lips. Shocked, she lurched away. "What do you think you're *doing?*"

He straightened abruptly, as though struck. "I thought…"

Mortified, she jerked on his hold and he let her go. "You were wrong, Doc! Once again, you misjudged me!" He had, hadn't he? She'd never had any intention of kissing the man. Had she?

It was one thing to engage in a little mental exercise, but quite another to act on it. Dana Vanover was no femme fatale. She was a lonely, frustrated librarian who was obviously not thinking straight. "It's been a long day," she muttered. "I'm going to bed."

"In a minute, Angel," he muttered.

With stunning suddenness, he claimed her lips with his. She didn't know if it was the unexpectedness of the act, or the kiss, that threw her senses into a wild swirl, but she was instantly dizzy. Her arms tingled with the need to snake up and curl around his neck, but she couldn't lift them. They hung at her sides like limp pasta. Her legs were hardly more substantial. If he hadn't crushed her in his arms, she would have been sprawled on the floor in a dead faint.

His mouth moved hungrily, searching, demanding a response. *Oh, Lord! This couldn't be happening.* Desperately she tried to hate his taste, his texture, tried to struggle, but nothing happened. But the kiss. The kiss went on, deliriously and beautifully on....

With a sinking feeling, Dana realized that there was nothing to hate about the experience—and everything to adore. This veterinarian was as talented at kissing as he was at healing—and leaping tall obstacles in a single bound. Was there nothing he couldn't do?

His lips cajoled and beguiled, flooding her limbs with new energy. Unable to help herself, she began to kiss him back. Her arms stole upward to encircle his neck, relishing the hard heat of his flesh. Her lips parted, surrendering to his lusty petition for a deeper, more exhilarating taste.

She moaned against his mouth, her heart soaring even as her brain recoiled. What was she doing? Where did she think this would lead?

With the quickness of a lightning bolt, the kiss ended, and Dana was set away. She found herself swaying unsteadily, staring into Sam's face. She blinked, trying to get him in focus.

"*Now* you may go to bed." He folded his arms across his chest. "I don't know what that little performance was all about, but..." A muscle flexed in his jaw. "Don't come on to me again, unless you're prepared to get what you ask for."

She gaped, appalled. She *had* asked for that kiss—at the very least! In fact, she'd practically said, *Do me, Doc!* Was she deranged?

His jaw shifted from side to side. "I'll see you at seven-thirty in the clinic. Don't be late."

Before she could find her voice, he stepped into his room and soundlessly closed the door.

SAM DIDN'T SLEEP very well. Hell, he didn't sleep at all. What had come over him last night? He *knew* better. With a curse, he threw off the sheet and tugged on a pair of shorts. It was still dark, but he might as well get up. He had a full day ahead of him in the clinic. He took a step toward the door, then stopped, peering over his shoulder.

The woman.

With a burdened exhale, he silently entered the bathroom, then turned the knob that led to her room. He was surprised when he met with no resistance from a barricade. As he cracked the door, he told himself he was merely making sure she was there, asleep.

She was. She lay on her side, facing him, wearing a T-shirt of his. A trace of pale, bare hip was exposed to his view. She looked sweet in repose. Even innocent—in a cruelly sexual way. His gut tightened and he scowled, irritated that his body didn't react to her with even the slightest degree of antagonism.

From his vantage point he counted three cats in bed with her. One that looked surprisingly like Pouncer, rested its head on her ankle. A second, he couldn't see very well, lay behind her on her pillow. The third, snow-white and definitely Mr. Chan, was curled against her breast. She'd draped an arm across it, cuddling the lucky little bastard close.

He winced at the contrary thought and backed out, stealthily closing the door.

Angelfish had made a *big* mistake when she came on to him last night. He had to admit, she was good. Even knowing she was a liar and most likely a career criminal, she'd made him lose focus for a minute. He didn't know what the hell she was planning, but he didn't intend to get sucked into her trap. All she'd accomplished with her female razzle-dazzle was to firm up his suspicions and put him on full alert.

A nagging inner voice taunted, *That's not all she firmed up, Gomer.*

"Oh, shut up!" He flinched as he bounded down the stairs. "Hell," he muttered. "She's got me talking to myself!"

THE NEXT TWO DAYS were pure hell for Dana, forced to spend countless hours in close proximity to Sam. Practically attached to his hip, she assisted him in doctoring Beena's precious felines. Every minute his scent taunted and the memory of his kiss grew more and more troubling. It seemed as though she'd been required to look into those deceptively sleepy eyes, tens of thousands of times, only to see distrust and hostility flare in their depths.

On the up side, she stopped heaving her cookies by Monday afternoon. The other ''up'' thing was, today was Beena's birthday, and there would be a party tonight. Dana had become very fond of the eccentric woman, and looked forward to their Bingo games after dinner. One surprising thing Dana discovered about herself was that she enjoyed having a cat curled in her lap and was starting to feel almost naked without one.

She still thought Mona was extremely weird. She looked a little too much like the living dead for Dana's peace of mind. But she did smile every so often. An eerie sight to say the least. Dana almost expected to see Dracula fangs when she bared her teeth.

Madam Rex had been the antithesis of what Dana expected. The woman looked more like a stock broker or a real-estate agent than a cat astrologist, in her linen suits, three-inch heels and perfectly coifed, platinum chignon. Though on the surface Madam Rex looked cool and businesslike, she jabbered like a magpie, and had a guffaw so high and screechy it wrenched birds out of trees and into frenzied flight.

"Shall we go, Angel?"

Dana was jerked from her reverie by Sam's hand at her elbow. The dratted suspicious doctor escorted her everywhere she went. On the surface, to the staff, he looked like a gentleman. But deep in his eyes she read the true story. He didn't trust her as far as he could fling her.

She glanced his way. "I thought I'd stay in the clinic. With a couple of discarded swabs and suture thread I figured I'd build myself a time bomb."

"Didn't MacGyver do that once?"

"Who's MacGyver?" She didn't know if amnesiacs were supposed to have gaping holes in their memories when it came to TV reruns, but she was taking no chances.

His lips quirked in a cynical smile. "Touché." She felt herself being propelled toward the exit as Sam nodded a friendly goodbye to the night shift. "So, who are you coming to the party as?"

She frowned, confused. "What?"

"The birthday party. We're supposed to come as our favorite singer."

She studied him, her frown intensifying. "You're joking."

A wry brow rose. "Beena's birthday party is no joking matter."

"Who are you coming as?"

"Elvis."

Dana stared.

"No cracks." He steered her toward the stairs. "It's Beena's request. She loves Elvis."

"Even though he's a man?"

"Beena thinks he had more whimsy than most men."

"He had more something, but I wouldn't have called it whimsy." She gave him a serious once-over. "I suppose you look a little like Elvis, around the kisser, *lips!*" She bit her tongue, wishing she could cut the mutinous thing out. Talk about Freudian slips! That had not only been a slip, it had been the corset, cincher, bustle and pantaloons! Obviously her rigorous attempts over the past forty-eight hours to banish memories of those gifted lips had been an unqualified failure.

Sam made no comment, but his grip at her elbow tightened. No words were necessary for her to understand that the subject was not his favorite, either.

"I don't think I'll go to the party," she said once she got her voice back. "I'm worn out."

"You're going."

She shot him a look of incensed indignation. "You're not my keeper!"

"Dream on, Angelfish." He eyed her levelly. "I am your keeper, your shadow, your worst nightmare." They climbed the stairs side by side, his pace deliberate, as though he intended to sustain his intimidation for as long as possible. "Until you give me a solid, credible reason to trust you, I'm going to hound your every move."

She glared at him. Unfortunately her stupid power experiment the other night had made things worse. "You haven't trusted me since I washed up on the beach!" she said.

"Yes, I did. For about five minutes."

She dropped her gaze, unsettled by the intensity of his stare. "I wouldn't hurt your aunt," she murmured, too tired to fight. "Never in a thousand years."

"I've heard that before." They reached the top of the staircase and he shifted her to face him. "Look at me."

She had no intention of obeying his barked order, yet she found herself lifting her gaze. She glowered, stiff and unhappy.

His lips crooked in a mocking grin. "Because of me, my aunt lost something very valuable a few years ago. I'd taken over the hiring of her staff, thinking she wasn't business-like enough." He laughed, the sound caustic. "I knew so much. I saw right through to people's souls." His blue eyes flashed fire. "I hired a sweet little thing as a housemaid. Barely eighteen and right off the farm, she looked as naive as Kansas corn. A month later she disappeared with—something Beena treasured." His nostrils flared, and Dana had the feeling he was experiencing a stab of self-recrimination.

"Beena kept me and my dad from starving after the accident. I owe her everything. If it weren't for her I wouldn't be a veterinarian today. I don't know what I'd be—or where."

"Accident?" She heard the word as she spoke it.

He winced. "Hurricane. The shelter wall collapsed. My mother, my little sister..." He gritted his teeth and looked away, as though trying to escape a painful vision.

"They were killed?"

He didn't speak for a moment. "My father was a paraplegic after that. We had no insurance. Beena paid his medical bills for the rest of his life. And how did I repay her? By sending a thief to her on a silver platter.'' His voice lashed out, but Dana detected the crack of emotion. ''It won't happen again, Angel.'' His stare was hard. ''Do you understand?''

So they'd both been fooled by a skillful con, huh? She experienced a pinprick of empathy, and had to fight the urge to hug him. No wonder he was so suspicious of her and so protective of his aunt. Dana's anger melted away. She wondered for a quick moment if she could trust him, tell him why she was here. But as quickly as the thought struck, she batted it back.

She didn't dare. In a little over a week she would be free to come clean without fear that Tate could still pull off his scam. ''I—I see,'' she said softly, then indicated her door. ''This is where I get off.''

She moved toward the entrance, noting that his hand remained on her elbow. He wasn't giving her an inch. That was fine, for now. She'd already done all the sabotage that needed doing. Unless the doc decided to leave before the two weeks were up. In that case, he'd find his boat suddenly dead in the water. Meanwhile, she opted to work on *not* inciting any more distrust in the man than she already had.

At her door she arranged her face placidly. ''I've thought of a singer I can come to the birthday party as, who's even more whimsical than Elvis.''

He pressed down on the handle, unlatching her door and pushing it open. ''I'm locking you in. Be ready at seven.''

Dana's animosity flared in spite of her vow not to aggravate him. She was getting pretty weary of his dictates. ''Flatterer,'' she cooed, batting her lashes. ''I bet you say that to *all* the hostages.'' With a sarcastic smirk, she stepped inside her room and slammed the door.

SAM SAT BESIDE his great-aunt at a long table on the patio. The guests consisted of all staffers not specifically on duty. They laughed and chattered, enjoying Beena's birthday rose petal ice cream. Dinner had consisted of rose petal sandwiches and rose hip tea. Sam ate nine of the little triangular mouthfuls, but felt as if he could still down a couple of burgers. Visiting an island full of women and trying to subsist on finger food had its drawbacks. He took another bite of the pink-tinted ice cream blended with real petals, striving *not* to follow Angel's every move.

She looked cute in her makeshift Carmen Miranda costume. She wore a bright purple-and-yellow-print shirt, tied beneath her breasts. A pair of mauve silk boxers served as modest underwear. A green-and-blue-striped woven table covering, tied at her waist, became a long skirt with a side slit. Sam had no idea how, but she'd managed to attach a bunch of bananas to the top of the jade towel wrapped like a turban around her head. Bunches of grapes hung from the towel for earrings.

Damn it if she hadn't won first prize in the costume contest. Oh, sure, she'd tried not to accept the little ruby and gold drop necklace, but Beena—being Beena—had insisted. He took another bite of his ice cream and eyed the blonde with misgiving. She'd certainly wormed her way into his great-aunt's heart. It didn't hurt that she'd volunteered to cut the tunafish cake. He watched her, placing china plates full of the stuff on the patio surface for the swarming cats.

"Angel's such a dear child," Beena said, drawing Sam from his morose preoccupation with a woman he didn't trust but craved like hell.

Sam glanced at his aunt. "I'm not sure about her. She's not being open with us."

"Sammy, love, she has amnesia." Beena placed a tiny, cool hand on his arm. In a black turtleneck and slacks, and with her hair plastered down around her face and tinted chocolate brown, she looked like a withered, smaller-than-scale Beatle. Sam wasn't sure if she was supposed to be Ringo or Paul, and decided not to incite her exasperation by asking.

"Sammy, love, how can our Angel be open when her mind is closed, even to her?"

Sam frowned. "I don't believe she has amnesia."

Beena looked bewildered for a second, then tittered. "Silly Sammy." She patted his arm lovingly. "Of course she does." She fluttered a beringed hand in the blonde's direction. "Look at that costume! Carmen Miranda was from Cuba! Doesn't that make you realize Angel is subconsciously trying to get her memory back?"

"I don't think Carmen Miranda was from Cuba. I think she was from Brazil."

"Pish tosh." Beena waved off his correction. "Spanish is Spanish."

"Unless it's Portuguese," he murmured.

"What did you say, love?"

"I think Portuguese is spoken in Brazil."

Beena rolled her eyes. "Well, how would Angel know that? She has—"

"Amnesia, I know," Sam said, defeated. He'd never figured out how to fight his aunt's non-logic.

Beena leaned nearer to her grand-nephew. "Speaking of Cuba..." She tittered again, lifting a hand to hide her mouth from the others sitting around the table. "I foiled the border patrol, yesterday."

Sam experienced a twinge of unease, but had no idea why. Her comment made absolutely no sense. He bent down so he could hear her better. "Did you say something about a border collie?" He hoped.

"No, Sammy!" Beena grinned broadly. "The border *patrol*. I foiled them!"

Sam shook his head, still not getting it. "What border are you talking about?"

"The United States, Sammy. Don't be dim!" She pinched his cheek, giving him her why-can't-you-be-more-whimsical look. "Yesterday while I was down on the dock, fishing with Whiskers and Sweetmeat, they swung by in one of those sleek 'Go Fast' boats."

"They?"

"Two border patrol men."

"What made you think they were I.N.S.?"

She looked confused. "I.N.S.? What's I.N.S.?"

"Immigration and Naturalization Service—Border patrol."

Beena nodded and smiled in understanding. "Ah." She took another bite of her ice cream. It seemed like a year before she swallowed. "Well, these patrol officers asked me if we'd seen or heard of anybody strange on the island."

Sam felt peculiarly apprehensive. "Did they specifically mention a woman?"

Beena shook her head. "No, but I knew they were asking about Angel."

Sam remembered the "foiled" remark and a knot tightened in his gut. "What did you tell them?"

She giggled. "Well, naturally I told them this was a very small, private island and with our security system, nobody strange could possibly be on our island."

That was a matter of debate. Everybody on the island was a little strange. He frowned at her. "You told them that?"

"Of course, Sammy." She shook her head at him at though he were a lost cause in the whimsy arena. "I wouldn't think of being a party to sending that sweet child back. Besides, she's not *strange* at all." She giggled at her little witticism.

Sam closed his eyes and counted to ten. What had his aunt done? At the very least Angelfish was truly an amnesiac who's family was desperately searching for her. At worst, those men were cops hunting down a criminal. "Did they show you badges?"

She made a scrunched-up face. "No, silly. They didn't have the time. I suppose if I'd told them Angel was here, they'd have produced the badges so they could drag her away. But why get all official when they think there's nobody to drag off?"

Sam exhaled long and low. *Damn.* "What did they say?" he asked, trying to keep the exasperation out of his voice.

Beena lifted skinny shoulders and let them fall. "Nothing. Just frowned a little, looked at each other, gunned the engine of their boat and phffff-fffft—" she wagged her fingers toward the sea "—they were gone."

Sam stared, disbelieving. "But, Aunt Beena..."

She patted his cheek. "Not another word, Sammy. You're getting worry lines and you're way too young for that." She stood, then watched him for a moment, her expression going serious. "You're still eaten up about that maid who stole dear Norman's gift to me." Her lips pressed into a thin, melancholy smile.

The sight of that sad, hard-fought smile, the glitter of memory in her eyes, caused Sam more agony than any ranting or raving could ever do. "Sammy. The ring was merely a symbol of his affection. If he hadn't died on the eve of our wedding..."

She faltered, freshening her smile with obvious difficulty. "I still can't believe that the darling, sweet man had already made out his will to leave me his entire fortune. Such a sweet thing to do." She sighed. "I'll always have the memory—of the world's most whimsical man. The ring..."

She shook her head and gently stroked his temple. Sam could tell she was making an effort to recover her voice. "Don't let the theft of that ring make you jaded, Sammy, love. I don't blame you." She licked her fingers, then repaired the Elvis lock on his forehead. "I could never be mad at my darling Elvis. You're human, so you're not perfect. Though I rarely admit it out loud, I'm not quite perfect, myself."

She glanced at Dana, chatting with Bertha, who was dressed like the head-bustingest Madonna Sam could possibly imagine. "I suppose our Angel isn't perfect, either." She gave Sam a fond slap on the cheek. "But I'd throw my lucky brooch into the sea before I'd believe that sweet girl is out to bilk me of a thing." She stroked the diamond kitty pen on her shirt. Sam knew it was Beena's other most treasured gift from her late, everlastingly lamented fiancé, lost so long ago. "Now stop fretting and have fun. It's my birthday, and I insist!"

He frowned and opened his mouth to speak, but Beena shushed him. "Go over there and get that pile of silk scarves by the door, Sammy."

He started to protest, to insist Beena be on her guard, but she gave him a shove. "Go— *go!* Daylight's wasting."

He passed by Madam Rex, costumed as Dolly Parton, and Mona, a remarkable likeness for a totally wasted Mick Jagger. The two women relaxed on lounge chairs, munching rose petal desserts. Mona's baby iguanas clung to the dirty-white T-shirt that hung loosely over her scrawny chest.

With great reluctance, he peered toward the table that supported the big tuna sheet cake slathered with cream cheese icing. The surface of the table teemed with cats that had decided to forgo the nicety of a plate.

Bertha and Angelfish backed away in self-defense, laughing as the painstakingly decorated kitty dessert became trampled hash. Sam shook his head. He'd be treating more than a few cases of tuna hangover tomorrow.

He heard Angel laugh. The sound seemed unnaturally loud amid the din of thirty-odd party-goers and carousing cats. Irritated that his brain seemed bent on singling her out by sight *and* sound, Sam snatched up the scarves. He had no idea what his aunt had in mind. Knowing her, it could be anything from making silk kites, to using them as blindfolds for a game of pin-the-tail-on-everybody. He returned to Beena's side as she began to tap on a water goblet to get everybody's attention.

"Okay, okay. Dinner's over," Beena shouted. "Let the games begin!"

Sam felt her take his arm and hug it to her. "Since it's my birthday, I make the rules, as usual. And, as usual, I have complete sway over who wins."

She tugged one scarf from Sam's fingers and held it high. "First, we're going to have a three-legged race. Each team will have three scarves with which to tie their legs together— one leg per team member, that is—at the thigh, knee and ankle." She cleared her throat importantly. "After much reflection, I have settled on these two-man teams. There shall be no substitutions! My word is law. I have the list right here." She flipped her hand so a piece of paper snapped open. "Without further ado—team one, Bertha and Eartha. Team two, Madam Rex and Mona...'' As Beena read down the list, Sam scanned it. He read the bad news, and peered at Angel, catching her frowning his way.

He sensed she dreaded what he already knew. Angelfish-of-the-wrinkled-brow would be his partner in the three-legged race.

He wasn't any happier about it than she looked. The last thing he needed was to be tied bodily to the woman. Ever since he'd grabbed her and kissed her two nights ago, he'd been furious with himself. He'd known *then* that getting hot and bothered for a con artist was mega *stupid*. So, what had he done? He'd grabbed the woman and kissed the hell out of her. He gritted his teeth, forcing back the notion that it had been the purest sensual experience of his life. Damn it.

Damn her!

''Team eight, Angel and Sammy.''

Sam saw her wince, making it obvious she was no more thrilled than he. For some grotesquely absurd reason, that fact pricked his pride. In a surge of annoyance at her for making him crazy, he flashed his most sardonic grin.

She squeezed her eyes shut and mouthed something. He had a hunch it wasn't "Hallelujah!"

CHAPTER SEVEN

DANA MANAGED TO MAKE IT through dinner
and dessert without saying a word to Sam. She
knew it wasn't the best way to make herself
seem less dishonest, but she also knew Sam
was so suspicious she could probably tell him
the truth, and he would only stare at her with
that I-wasn't-born-yesterday scowl.

Why Beena paired her with Sam for the
three-legged race was anybody's guess. Dana
would never have imagined the elderly woman
had cupid inclinations, but it was beginning to
look that way. How ironic! She and Sam were
about as likely to become a compatible pairing
as the Miami Dolphins and the Bolshoi Ballet.

She caught movement out of the corner of
her eye and shifted, wary. Oh, no! Here he
came. Elvis Sherlock Holmes, carrying three
scarves in his fist. It was a real shame he
looked so…whimsical. Yes, whimsical was a

173

better word for her to use than sexy, since she was about to be bound to him, and she was still trying to forget how he tasted.

He wore a loose white silk shirt, open midway down his chest, silver belt buckle, form-fitting white silk pants and white bucks. He wore his hair the way Elvis had, a heavy lock curled in the middle of his forehead. And just to make her totally nuts, a silver medallion hung from a heavy chain around his neck, flashing as he walked, drawing her attention to his chest, over and over and over.

She stood on the lawn near what had been determined to be the starting area. She shifted from foot to foot, glancing across the golf-green turf to where a couple of servants had been posted. A long strip of crepe paper stretched between them served as the finish line.

Sam came to a stop in front of her, giving her costume a quick once-over. Her heart fluttered maddeningly, but she told herself she didn't give a fig what he thought.

"May I have a banana?" he asked. "I'm starving."

She met his gaze as he plucked a grape from her earring and popped it into his mouth.

"Hey, you're eating my costume!"

"You're lucky you're not wearing steak and potatoes." He relieved her of another grape and popped it into his mouth.

"Didn't you eat dinner?" She knew very well he had. She'd caught herself peeking at him a time or two. Or six hundred. With a little more force than necessary, she yanked at a banana, only managing to slide the turban askew over her eyes. As she straightened the headdress, she succeeded in breaking a banana off the bunch.

Sam took it and began to peel. "Don't tell Beena, but as far as I'm concerned, rose petals are a poor substitute for food."

"I'll leave it out of my report," she wisecracked, looking him up and down. This getting-tied-together thing was a bad idea. She had to figure out a way to get out of it. But how? Maybe if she came up with a good enough argument? "This game is dangerous. You'll stomp all over my bare feet with your big shoes."

He took a bite of the banana, glanced at her, then at his shoes. "I'll take them off."

She grimaced. She'd wanted him to say something like, "Rather than ruin my look, let's forget the whole thing, *chiquita!*"

Scraping the heel of one shoe against the toe of the other, he stepped out of one white buck, then the other. He wagged his brows. "Okay?"

No, it wasn't okay! She thought fast. "You're too big to be my partner." She swept an arm out. "Beena partnered everybody else according to size. You outweigh me by a hundred pounds!"

He finished the banana and tossed the peel beside his shoes. "Yeah? You're the most Junoesque eighty-five-pound anorexic I've ever seen."

Junoesque? Librarian that she was, she knew it meant "stately," "majestic" and "statuesque," but she doubted the naive blonde with amnesia would know. She planted her fists on her hips. "Is that a crack?"

His eyes narrowed as he ambled to her side and butted a hard thigh against her bare leg. "This one okay?"

She backed off. "No."

He nodded and walked around to her other side. "This leg's covered by your skirt. You'll need to take it off?"

"Right after you take off your pants!" she snapped.

"Okay." He grinned and went for the belt buckle.

"No!" She exhaled heavily, then realized she needed to inhale. Her heart thudded stupidly. "Never mind." She touched her bare thigh. "This leg's fine."

He nodded matter-of-factly, and walked back around. "Stick it out."

She glared at him, but did as he ordered.

Once again, he pressed his thigh to hers. "Hold these." He thrust her two of the scarves. "I'll tie."

She clamped her jaws and reluctantly took the scarves. This was *not* happening!

His hand skimmed around her inner thigh and she gasped.

He glanced up. "What?"

She shook her head, swallowing. "Nothing."

He returned to his work, tying the scarf in a double knot.

"We'll never get that off!"

"Sure we will. Hold still." He grabbed another scarf and slid it around her knee. "Our knees don't quite come to the same place."

"No kidding, Sherlock."

He paused, seeming to study the situation. While he considered, he cupped the back of her knee in his palm. The contact was way too warm and bordered on suggestive.

"Would you just tie it, *please!*"

"Don't you want to win?"

"I don't even want to play."

He glanced at her, his gaze speculative. "You look like a player to me."

For some crazy reason, his comment seemed off-color. She crossed her arms in front of her. "I wouldn't know."

He grinned, and a quiver of wayward appreciation raced down her spine. "Right. The amnesia thing. It slipped my mind for a second."

"Just *tie*."

He went back to work, his fingers brushing, stroking and highly unsettling—a torrid counterpoint to the cool, airy silk.

After what seemed like a decade, he finished. They were bound together like a book— a huge, unhappy book from which pages couldn't be torn without bloodshed.

He straightened. "Put an arm around my waist." He slid his arm around her shoulders. "It'll keep us steadier."

She hesitated to unclench her arms from beneath her breasts. For two days he'd looked at her as if she were a rash he couldn't cure. Why was he being so agreeable? "You're awfully helpful."

His brows rose in a resigned shrug of sorts. "She's my aunt."

Dana could accept that. Sam was merely going along to please the woman he owed so much. With a small nod, she slipped an arm behind his back and around his waist.

"Okay, everybody!" Beena shouted from the sidelines. "I want all the partners to walk a little for practice." She looked at her watch. "You have five minutes!"

Dana heard the groan, then realized the sound came from her own throat.

Sam's low laugh rumbled through her, and she peered his way. He squeezed her shoulder. "Let's walk, Angelfish." He watched her for a minute while she glowered at him, then inclined his head. "On the count of three."

On three, Dana stepped out with her left foot as Sam propelled her right foot forward, leaving her upper torso trailing behind. She squealed as she began to fall. Sam's arm tightened around her, saving her toppling bacon.

"I meant, on three step forward with your *tied* leg."

She flicked him a withering glance. "Oh? You think reading your mind is that easy?" She was so irritated! Not because she'd almost fallen, but because being nestled against him ignited ever nerve in her body. Her pulse was behaving like that of an adolescent Elvis groupie lashed to The King himself. Unsettled, she snapped, "*I'll* count this time."

"That's all right, mama," he drawled Elvisly, glancing at her with twinkling bedroom eyes. "Remember, start with the tied—"

"One!" she shouted, dying for the game to be over. "Two! *Three!*"

This time they managed to take three whole steps before Dana reeled and clung to him bodily. "Wait! You're taking too big steps! I'm not six feet tall!"

"Hell, when we run—"

"If you don't shorten your stride, you'll be dragging my lifeless body behind you." She made quick work of righting herself. The last thing she needed to do was cling to the man! "Is that how you envisioned crossing the finish line?"

"I haven't really dwelled on it."

"Well, *dwell* a little."

"Smaller steps. Check." His jaws worked, and Dana could tell he was finding it more and more difficult to hide his irritation at being partnered with her—aunt or no aunt.

"On the count of three," she said.

He nodded, but didn't look her way.

After several more false starts, they got a rhythm going, and Dana finally felt comfortable with the three-legged thing, but not with her close proximity to Sam. He smelled delicious, and beneath the soft silk shirt, his taut flesh tormented her relentlessly.

As they came to a stumbling halt after their tenth practice walk, her turban was skewed over her eyes; she pushed it back. "Hasn't it been five minutes, yet?" Affliction was ripe in her tone. "It seems like five hours."

"If that was supposed to be a compliment, Angel, you need to work on your people skills."

His cheeky grin added fuel to the fires of her distress. She fought an urge to stick out her tongue, but remembered she'd presented that mutinous bit of anatomy to the doc far too liberally in the past twenty-four hours.

"One minute, people!" Beena blew a whistle to make sure she had their attention. "All teams, move to the starting line!"

"Thank heaven," Dana muttered.

"Okay, we start with the tied leg," he said. "All you have to do is hang on."

She shot him a perturbed look. "That's not what we practiced."

"We didn't practice running."

"We don't have to win, you know."

"It's in my nature to try." His lips crooking wryly. "Isn't it in yours?"

She shook her head, aggravated by his everlastingly sneaky interrogations. "Nice try, Doc. But as far as I know, I'm a loser, and lovin' it."

"Not today, you're not." He slid his hand from her shoulder, crooking it under her arm. His fingertips brushed the side of her breast. "When the race starts, grab my waist and hold on."

"Just be careful what *you* grab." She scooted his hand down her rib cage. He now embraced bare flesh, but the erogenous zoning was less consequential.

"On your mark!" Beena shouted. "Get set!"

Dana felt Sam's muscles tense. She knew at that instant she was out of her element if she had any illusions about keeping up with him. Why did she have to suffer this paralyzing insight a millisecond before Beena blew the starting whistle?

"Go!"

After the first jolting stride, Dana reflexively grabbed Sam around the waist and held on for dear life. The contest became a blur. Every so often her left foot connected with solid ground, but most of the time, she hung around Sam's body like a hundred and twenty-five pound sack of kumquats.

All of a sudden, they lumbered past a fluttering crepe paper tape. Dana had the vague sense they didn't break it. However that thought didn't linger long. Sam made a guttural noise, and the next instant she found her-self on the ground. Well, not quite. She was, more or less, on Sam.

"Whew!" He sucked in a gulp of air. "How much do you weigh, woman?"

She was sprawled half on his chest, her left leg thrown over his right. Coming up on one elbow she pushed her turban out of her eyes. "I weigh practically nothing. How *rude* of you to ask." Her smirk was smart-alecky. "Out of shape, Doc?" It gratified her that she could breath normally, while his chest heaved with his effort to take in deep drags of oxygen. "Want me to help you up?"

He frowned, lifted his head, then seemed to reconsider, relaxing back down in the grass. "Angelfish, have you ever seen a horse and wagon when the *wagon* was tired?"

She made a face, struggling to hide her amusement. She had no idea why she found this so funny, but she did. "I told you not to take such big steps. It's your fault." His arm was still around her; his fingers splayed over her bare torso. "By the way, did we win?"

"No, we didn't. Bertha and Eartha won. Probably because nobody had to *drag* anybody on their team."

"Maybe nobody took gigantic, dinosaurian strides, either."

"Dinosaurian, huh?" He tugged off her turban and tossed it aside.

"Hey!" She grabbed for it, but wasn't quick enough. "That's my tutti-frutti hat!"

"It's gone to tutti-frutti heaven. It might have helped if you'd actually been able to see."

"I could see! Part of the time...with one eye..." She couldn't hold back her grin any longer. "Okay, okay. I wasn't much help. So, where did we finish?"

"Second." He squinted, scrutinizing her. "Nice hair."

She ran a hand through the mess. "Second?" She mulled that over, stacking her hands on his chest and resting her chin on them. "Second seems good."

"Considering." His grin was teasing, his heavy-lidded gaze lazily erotic.

She took the bait, trying not to dwell on the fact that the hard length of his body was disconcertingly cozy. "*Considering* you took mutant Abominable Snowman steps."

"Considering I had a Volkswagen lashed to my leg."

She laughed, which was bizarre, since he'd just insinuated she weighed as much as a car! "So what do we win?"

"I hope, food." His hand slid from her rib cage to the middle of her back. Dana sensed he was letting go, and caught her breath in dismay. But he didn't quite relinquish his touch. His hand lingered at the small of her back.

She told herself she was stupid to be alarmed that he might take his hand away. She commanded her body to slip off, get away from his scent, his touch, but nothing happened. Some insubordinate imp in her brain had taken control of the cluster of cells regulating arm and leg function. She had no choice but to idle on top of him, grinning, sniffing, cuddling and—

Cuddling! Dana Vanover have you mislaid your mind?

Where had her good intentions gone—the ones where she'd vowed to shun physical male beauty, to look deeper into a man's soul to discover his worth? With a new sense of urgency, she shoved herself off, thudding onto her back with a *woof!* She closed her eyes and cursed herself for the pain her abrupt plunge caused.

"I can't give you many points for that dismount," Sam said.

By the time Dana steeled herself to peer at him, he'd come up on one elbow, his expression amused and quizzical.

She indicated their bound legs. "Just untie us, please."

He sat up and began to work the knots loose. After another minute she scooted to her elbows and glanced around, trying not to obsess over his warm fingers brushing against her leg. Strangely enough, two teams still hobbled toward the finish line. The rest were already over the finish line. Some sprawled, as she and

Sam. The rest standing, hanging on to each other, laughing so hard they were in tears.

Dana shifted to watch the last teams strive for the finish. One of the couples Dana recognized as part of the cleaning staff. The other team was Mona and Madam Rex. Mona virtually dragged her teammate, who kept crumbling to one knee and screeching, "Let me die! Let me die!" But Mona plodded on. Her gaunt features were a study in grim determination, the likes of which could only be found among the living dead, stiff-limbed and blank-eyed as they lurched from the grave to terrorize the living.

Dana couldn't stifle her giggle at the absurd sight.

The other team staggered across the finish line. Two seconds later so did Mona and a caterwauling Dolly Parton.

"There, you're free." Dana felt Sam's hand drop lightly over her knee. She jerked to face him. He lifted the hand and extended it. "Need help getting up?"

She shook her head and pushed up to stand. Rather than look at him, she shifted to watch Madam Rex and Mona. Madam Rex was shrieking something unintelligible as she hauled Mona to the ground and clutched her around the neck. The baby iguanas hopped off Mona's shoulders and scurried to safety.

"Oh, dear!" Dana envisioned murder most foul, and took a step in their direction.

Sam grasped her wrist. "They do this every year. It's tradition."

Dana stared at him. A grin tugged at his lips.

"You *lie!*" she said with a laugh.

His eyes lost their sparkle. "No, Angel. That's your department."

The remark was like a pinprick to a bubble, and the fun went out of the moment. Dana hiked her chin, but couldn't form a reply. Slipping from his grasp, she turned away. "I have a headache. I'm going to bed."

"What about your prize?"

"You eat it for me," she called.

"What if it's not food?"

"Even better!"

He didn't toss back anything caustic, and Dana took a relieved breath. She quickened her pace toward the patio steps.

"Get plenty of rest," he shouted. "The supply boat comes tomorrow."

She faltered, almost tripped. Tomorrow? Already? Her blood ran cold. There was no way on earth Sam would let that boat leave the island and *not* contact the coast guard.

How was she going to stop him?

CHAPTER EIGHT

SAM YANKED OFF HIS SHIRT and dropped down to hunker on the edge of his bed. A cat meowed its objection to being awakened and Sam glanced over his shoulder. "Sorry, Gargantua. Go back to sleep." He exhaled wearily and leaned forward, resting his forearms on his knees. "Damn it! I'm such a fool," he muttered.

It had been an hour since Angel left the party. His body still thrummed with the feel of her, lying on top of him, all curvy and soft. He mouthed a curse. If her plan was to slyly seduce him, make him let down his guard long enough for her to strike and disappear, she wasn't doing half bad.

He groaned and shoved his hands through his hair. What was the matter with him? Why did it seem this woman had taken something from deep inside him the first instant he laid eyes on her—something precious and essential—something he could never get back?

He didn't know much about love. His mother died when he was six, and his aunt had never married. Yet, he was well aware of Beena's abiding devotion to the man who died hours before their wedding was to have taken place. He knew Beena had loved Norman Gaylord so fiercely his death broke her heart. She'd never considered marrying anyone else.

Because of his aunt, Sam knew that a love-at-first-sight-and-forever kind of passion existed. How many times over the years had he heard about the day Norman Gaylord walked up to Beena, a petite nineteen-year old, and asked her out. She'd thought the wealthy entrepreneur was teasing, and she'd made a flip remark that she would be delighted, but she had to sell all the magazines in her stand first.

Norman had bought the stand, lock, stock, and barrel. In Beena's opinion, the romantic act had been exquisitely whimsical. They became engaged a week later.

It was a pleasant little yarn, but Sam had always assumed a man had *some* choice in the matter. Why, then, was he crazy-lost over a lying, conniving…

He shook his head and straightened, trying to get perspective. Hadn't he and Liza been a steady couple for a long time? They'd had their ups and downs, breakups and reconciliations, but they were basically compatible. Though marriage hadn't actually come up. It had been assumed that one day it would happen.

Even so, in these past four years he'd never felt that forever kind of tug in his gut. Lately he'd begun to think that the concept of love, as Beena described it, was romanticized fiction she'd conjured up over the years.

Now he knew differently. He saw the fire and spirit he'd looked for in Liza in a completely unexpected source. In Angel. Now he understood why marriage had never specifically come up, why he hadn't been able to make a permanent commitment to Liza. ''Because it was never love,'' he mumbled.

Nothing that even resembled love, or come close to the exhilarating wholeness he felt around a woman who didn't even have a name.

He sank to his back and stared up at the vaulted rafters, a dark realization chilling him.

Doctor Samuel Taylor—straight arrow, and champion of the world's suffering creatures—was in love with a fraud.

THE NEXT MORNING Dana caught a break on her way back to the clinic from the laundry, her arms loaded down with warm-from-the-dryer surgical greens. Bertha whizzed by with the news that the supply boat had docked.

Dana counted herself lucky that Sam kept his own council about his misgivings. Otherwise, Bertha wouldn't have babbled that news flash to *her* of all people. As innocently as she could, she nodded. "Oh? That's nice."

The ploy she'd painstakingly worked out would require split-second timing, and had to be pulled off immediately, before anybody called Sam on the intercom with the news. She'd been worrying over the scenario, trying

to work it out, since last night when Sam reminded her the supply boat was coming. To
pull off her plan, Dana only needed a screwdriver and a narrow window of opportunity.
Another lucky break happened when Sam left
the clinic for a few minutes to talk to his aunt.
There was her window!

Now, all she had to do was get Sam to co-
operate—just the tiniest bit.

As she reentered the clinic and closed the
door, Sam was pulling off rubber gloves and
dumping them in the trash. He dragged off his
mask and cap, eyeing her with the same troubled expression he'd aimed at her all morning.
The air was so tense Dana could almost feel it
pulsating around the room.

She shook herself. She mustn't get side-
tracked! It was now or never. She headed into
the storage room and stuffed the clean scrubs
onto a shelf at the back. Steeling herself for
her surprise attack, she screamed. Long and
loud.

"What the—"

She heard him, knew he'd be there in a second, so she turned away from the door, positioning herself precisely where she needed to be. She screamed again.

His scuffling footsteps told her when he'd entered the small room, so she flailed her hands, as though in panic.

"What is it?" he shouted.

"*Snake!*" She pointed vaguely beneath the lowest shelf to her left. "It went under there!"

He moved far enough inside the door for her to initiate Phase One. She stumbled backward, kicking the door with her heels until it clicked shut. All the while she pointed and screamed. "It's poisonous! It tried to bite me!"

Sam's expression was a mix of concern and skepticism. "How could a snake get—"

"There he is!" she cried, jabbing a finger at nothing in particular. "I saw his head for a second!"

Initiate Phase Two!

She leaped to the second shelf of the tall section of wooden shelving on her right and curled her fingers around the back of an upper shelf. Hanging off the front the way she was, her weight would topple the five foot by seven foot framework forward. She only hoped Sam had fast enough reflexes to jump farther back in the storeroom to get out of the way.

It began to pitch forward.

"Angel, don't—"

He didn't have time to finish before Dana initiated Phase Three. She leaped off the collapsing unit onto the shelving on the left. For good measure, she shrieked, "It's a coral snake! Save yourself!"

The horrendous crash of the first cabinet almost drowned out the last of her warning as she got a solid hold of the now-doomed section of shelving. This one was filled with paper supplies, rubber gloves, things that were heavy in bulk, but not breakable. It took effort to get it tumbling. And worse, Sam stepped in to try to keep it upright. Reacting quickly, she went into a hysterical act and swung wildly, knocking him away in time to keep him from ruining her plan.

The unit lurched forward. Dana sprang away, giving one last panicked scream for good measure, and did a soft-knee landing on the far side of the storeroom.

The second cabinet fell on top of the first with a deafening roar, followed by the rumble as supplies dropped, filtering through the first fallen shelves to the floor.

As soon as the collapse was a done deal, she clambered onto the top of the pile, reviving her shrieks.

"Damn it, Angel, *shut up!*"

She only had one more phase to complete. Picking up a clipboard, she wielded it like a weapon. "Climb up!" she cried. "Climb up before it gets you!" She held the clipboard over her head with both hands. "Can coral snakes climb? If I see it, I'll *wham* it!" She swung the board forward, praying she was directly under the light bulb.

She heard a small pop, and the place fell into darkness. She'd hit the bulb on the first try. Glass tinkled onto the ruins, not far in front of her. Though the place was black as tar, from the sound, she didn't think Sam had been close enough to get hit.

"What happened!" she yelled, adding just the right hint of a moan. *"Sam?"* She shut up. Her job was done.

When there was no sound for a few seconds, she manufactured a sniffle. "Sam? Are you there?"

"Damn it, where else would I be?"

So far, so good. She pulled her lips between her teeth to keep from grinning. It was very dark, but he might have excellent night vision. "Are you okay?"

"I'm in better shape than the stock room."

"You'd better climb up here, so the snake can't—"

"If there ever was a snake, it's a pancake now."

"What do you mean, *if* there ever was a snake!" Her indignation echoed around the small room, a wondrous likeness of the real thing.

"We're deep in the castle. A snake couldn't make it all the way in here undetected."

"I saw it!"

"Okay, okay. We can debate that later. Right now, we have bigger problems." He paused. "Where are you?"

"I'm—I'm standing on the...stuff."

"Rubble?"

She swallowed a giggle. She was horrible to do this to him. But a lot was at stake. "Uh-huh."

"It's dangerous, especially in the dark. You'd better get off."

"But—what if the snake..."

"Will you give it a rest?" She heard footsteps, then a bang. "*Ouch*. Okay. I'm at the edge. Come to me and I'll help you down."

"Are your arms out?"

"Yes." He sounded as though he was talking with his teeth gritted.

She bent to feel her way with her hands. Then realized she still held the clipboard. She dropped it and it clattered down the four feet of piled shelving to smack against the floor.

"What was that?"

"Just something I was holding. Are you sure your arms are out?"

"I'll check." He sounded exasperated. "Yeah, they're out. Come on."

She felt her way along the back edge of the shelving as though she were crouched on a tightrope. One hand skimmed the edge to her left, for balance. She wagged her right arm in front of her. "I don't feel you."

"Keep coming."

Finally she made contact. "Is that your arm?"

"Does it *feel* like an arm?"

Oh, Lord! She snatched her hand away. "Uh…actually—"

"Hold still," he cut in. "I'll find you."

"No—no. I can do this." She felt higher, and ran into something. "Is that you?" She prided herself at the dumbness of her question.

"No, it's Laurence Sterne."

Laurence Sterne? He was being sarcastic, but why pick the name of a long-dead British novelist? Dana was crazy about Sterne's *Tristram Shandy,* and wondered if she and

Sam had a love for his writing in common, but supposed she would never know. "Sterne?" she asked, manufacturing a puzzled tone. "Is that the shock jock guy?" She forced a giggle as if going along with his joke. "Well, Mr. Sterne, fancy meeting you here."

"It's a small storeroom. Can you find my other hand?"

"I think so." She let go with her balancing hand and waved it around to make contact. When they connected, she vaulted onto him, encircling his waist with her legs. "You don't mind, do you?" she asked. "I'm afraid of snakes."

He stumbled a step backward before his arms came around her. Clearly he hadn't expected her to clobber him with her whole body. "Good Lord, you could warn a guy."

"I'm sorry, Sam." She clung to his neck, her cheek brushing his ear. "I figured you knew what I'd do."

"In the past few minutes I've been pretty clueless about that."

She strangled a laugh. "I can't see a thing. Are there candles in here?"

"On the back shelf, I think."

"Take me back there. What about matches?"

"There should be a box."

"Okay, let's go." She tapped his butt with her feet. "Giddy-up."

"You're in a fine mood for somebody who barely escaped death by snakebite, was nearly crushed by five hundred pounds of shelving, and who has single-handedly destroyed my stock room. Your resilience amazes me."

There was that nasty suspicion in his tone again. Surely he didn't think she could have planned all—well, okay, she *had* planned it. But surely, he couldn't *think* she had! She worked hard at sounding contrite. "I'm sorry, Doc. I guess I'm in shock."

"If this is shock for you, I'm afraid to see what having a good time looks like."

He turned with her toward the back of the storeroom. She thought silently, *At least I didn't have to demolish all the shelves. Be happy about that.*

"You know, Angel, either you're the luckiest clumsy woman alive, or you're one of the Flying Wallendas."

She wasn't thrilled with the direction this conversation was taking. Why couldn't the man assume something was an accident with her? Why did he always have to believe she was lying and scheming?

Maybe because you've done nothing but lie and scheme since you met the guy, her mind charged. She told her mind to mind it's own business, then said aloud, "Uh...candles? Which side?"

"I'm backing up to them. Reach out, they should be at shoulder level."

She felt around. "Found them! Now hold me tight." She squeezed her legs more firmly around his waist. "I have to let go with both arms to light these."

"Why don't I let you down?" He sounded as if he was under a strain.

"Am I heavy?" She turned slightly, and felt his breath on her lips. A quiver of longing coursed through her body, but she fought it.

"In a way," he said.

"What about the snake?"

"I'll carry the snake."

She laughed, unable to stop herself. "That's funny, Doc."

"I'm letting you down."

"*No!* I'm lighting a match."

He muttered something, but Dana couldn't make it out. She had a feeling that it was just as well. With the strike of a match they had the miracle of light. Dana blinked, amazed by how bright the flicker of one tiny flame could seem in a pitch- dark room. Hurriedly, she held it to the wick of a chunky beeswax candle, then another. Before she blew out a second match, four candles illuminated the darkness. At least the darkness in the immediate vicinity.

And Sam's eyes—liquid and sensual in candlelight. She had a hard time compelling her gaze to the door, barely visible at the far end of the room.

In the waiting silence, Dana surrendered to the lure of Sam's face. She sensed a hard-fought reserve in his eyes, and sadness. Before she could be positive what she witnessed hadn't been a trick of the light, his lashes slipped to half mast, obscuring his thoughts.

She felt the heavy thud of his heart, and his scent seemed to be all around her. Why hadn't she foreseen that her ploy would require that they be stuck in close proximity for who-knew-how-long? The stillness grew electrified, and a trembling thrill raced through her. The impulse to move that tiny distance toward him, to taste his lips again, was almost a tangible entity, growing larger. Taking over.

She struggled to get herself under control. Faking a laugh, she searched for some way to funnel her thoughts to things that didn't involve kissing him. "Uh—this could be romantic—with the right two people." She cringed. *Yeah, that's funneling your thoughts, idiot!*

He squinted, looking as though he was in pain. "Unclench your legs, Angel. We need to get out of here."

A jolt of regret hit her, and she forced herself to look away before she did anything even more stupid. "Sure, okay." She let go. When her feet were beneath her, he released her and stepped away. It couldn't have been any clearer that he had no desire to linger in her arms—or her legs—if he'd painted the words Go Away! on his forehead.

Turning his back, he rested an arm on the shelf with the candles. After a few seconds he ran a hand through his hair.

"Are you okay?" she asked, wondering at his hesitation. The sport had gone out of her ruse. She was too aware of him, too in need of throwing her arms around his neck and begging for his kisses. How could she be such a selfish, manipulative fool?

She'd done nothing but maneuver this man since she'd met him, and now she wanted to use him to ease her sexual frustrations. What a rat she was! "I—I didn't strain anything, did I?" She truly hoped she hadn't caused him physical damage, too.

He cleared his throat and turned toward the shelf. "I'm fine. Just thinking how to get out of here." He picked up a candle and faced her, but his glance went to the door. "Looks like the shelves are blocking the exit. They have to be lifted out of the way."

She scrunched up her face as though trying to grasp that. "You mean, we can't get out?"

"Not without work." He looked at her. "How strong are you?"

"I—I think I wrenched something." She rubbed her shoulder, trying to look pitiful. It wouldn't do to lose everything she'd accomplished by going soft now. "But I'll do what I can."

He didn't look like a happy man. "Hold the candle." He thrust it at her. "And stay out of the way."

She nodded meekly, hoping he couldn't wrestle the shelves back against the wall too quickly. She had no idea how long that supply boat would be docked on the island, and could only pray nobody would come looking for them. In all the time she'd assisted in the clinic, they'd had few visitors. Not even cats. Most associated the antiseptic smell with negative experiences and steered clear.

Sam turned his back on her, planting fists on hips. He studied the situation, his heavy exhale revealing volumes about his mood.

She held the candle a little higher, and backed up a step. "Okay, now what?"

"I'm thinking."

Fifteen minutes later Sam had single-handedly bullied the shelves into place. He'd taken off his scrub shirt; his chest and back glistened from exertion. Dana had a hard time witnessing that gorgeous torso in action. Drat her hide! Why hadn't this possibility crossed her shriveled little mind?

He was well-built as it was, but bulging pecs and quads and—well, *bulging,* those various muscle groups drove her to the brink of promiscuity. She'd never had an urge to physically attack a man before, but if Sam had taken one more minute—*No! Thirty more seconds*—to get those shelves upright, she would have jumped him and had her way with him, right in the middle of two gross of Q-Tip swabs.

"Okay. We're out of here," he said, yanking her from her seriously depraved stupor.

She snapped her shoulders back and gave a hasty nod, avoiding looking at his glistening muscles, hard and distinct and alluring by candlelight. "Right, uh, good."

She could see well enough to step around and over the debris to get to the door. Sam got there first and turned the knob. It dropped off in his hand. "What in the…"

This last bit of business wasn't a particularly satisfying victory for Dana, but necessary. *Thank you, Daddy, for making me self-sufficient!*

She leaned forward, holding out the candle to put more light on Sam's handful of doorknob. She gasped, for show. "Why did you do that, Doc?"

With the speculative lift of a brow, he peered at her.

DANA STOOD IN THE SHOWER under a steady spray of warm water. She felt dirty, and she feared all the water in the world couldn't make her feel clean. She'd been as unscrupulous as Tate in her treatment of Sam and Beena.

She pressed her forehead against the cool tiles. Could she ever forget Sam's expression once he'd managed to get the door open, only to discover the supply boat had been and gone? He'd looked at her with such explosive rage, she was surprised the power of it hadn't blasted her through a wall. During the entire week she'd hid out on the island, she had never had a worse minute than that one, staring back at him, trying to appear the wide-eyed innocent.

She heard a sob, dismayed to discover she was crying. She pressed her hand over trembling lips, choking back the forlorn sound. Sam was on the other side of the bathroom door, hopefully, asleep. It was late. She'd avoided him for as much of the afternoon as she could. Played bingo after dinner with Beena, Eartha and one of the off-duty kitchen maids. She'd even gone so far as to take a circuitous route to her bedroom to dodge him.

Looking into Sam's eyes had become a painful experience she didn't care to repeat any more than necessary.

He'd ensconced himself in his office the rest of the day, no doubt clearing up the mess. She should have helped, but it was obvious he didn't want her around. Every glance he shot her flashed his antipathy. It was as though he were saying, *Just because I can't prove it, doesn't mean I don't know what you've done!*

She choked back another sob at the irony of her situation. To escape dire straits in which she'd been lied to and used, she was having to lie to and use these people. Regardless, she had to keep up the pretense. Sam was so angry now, he would probably report her to the coast guard simply because he thought she deserved whatever she got.

Even if she broke down and told him everything, she couldn't prove it. Why should he believe her confession wasn't merely another ploy to get him to pity her, to pull him off his guard? She'd dug herself such a deep hole, she was stuck with digging it a little deeper.

She promised herself, as soon as the two weeks were up, she would tell them the truth. She had a feeling Beena would forgive her. But Sam? Why should he? Dana could never forgive Tate, even if he reformed this very day and came crawling back to her. She would never trust him again. Why should Sam ever feel he could trust her after what she'd put him through?

What difference did it make? After the deadline, she would tell them the facts and go on with her life. Sam and Beena would go on with theirs. End of story.

She turned off the water and grabbed the towel she'd slung over the top of the glass stall. Patting herself dry, she stepped out onto the bathroom rug, squeezing excess water from her hair.

Wrapping the towel around her, she opened her door and stumbled to a dead stop.

A huge green monster stared back at her!

Dana and the scaly reptile stood stock-still for a few seconds, each apparently startled to see the other. At last, the beast opened its mouth and made a threatening noise, snapping her out of her paralysis. Whirling on her heel, she sprinted through the bathroom, slamming into Sam's room.

It was dark, but she hit the bed on the run. A big cat leaped off and squeezed under the bed as she scrambled up next to Sam. Squatting on her knees, she shoved at his shoulder, urgently whispering, ''Sam! *Sam!* There's a dragon in my bedroom!'' She shoved harder, trying to wedge herself under and behind him.

''What?'' He sounded groggy. His eyes fluttered open and he lolled his head in her direction, clearly half asleep. ''A what?''

''A Komodo dragon! A man-eater! It tried to bite me!'' He squinted, coming up on one elbow. She squirmed further behind him. ''Kill it, Sam!'' Looking confused, he pushed up to sit, and she scrambled to squat behind his back, pointing over his shoulder. ''It may have already eaten the cats!''

He shifted to better see her, his glance sliding down to take in the scrap of terry. When his gaze lifted, something in his eyes, something hot, yet inexplicably poignant, sent a surge of fire along her pulses. She sucked in a quivery breath.

He frowned and ground out a curse. "A Komodo dragon tried to bite you?"

She nodded vigorously. "I—I think that's what it is."

"Not a coral snake, this time?"

She shook her head. "Too big. This is really *big*, with legs! It roared at me and—bared hideous *fangs!*"

"Fangs..." he muttered, running a hand through his hair. He looked frustrated and cuddly. If Dana hadn't been so overwrought, she would have found him unbearably charming. Sadly, this wasn't the time, or the man, to find charming—especially while she was wearing nothing but a towel.

"Aren't you going to do anything?" she pleaded.

"You know what, Angelfish?" Muscles bunched in his jaw and he looked as if he might be counting to ten. "This game has quit being fun for me."

She stared, openmouthed. "Don't you believe me?"

"What's really going on?" he asked. Even dubious and irritated and frustrated, whatever his major emotion was, he was gorgeous. Dana's heart did an appreciative flip-flop, amazing her to discover she could be scared and aroused at the same time. "Why are you *really* here—in a towel?"

She grabbed his shoulders, then thought better of it and let go. "I'm telling the truth!"

He pursed his lips, plainly trying to remain composed. "Okay. You want me to go in there, is that it?"

"Yes! Go. Kill it."

"There'd better be something in there, and I don't mean falling roof beams."

"There is!" She shoved on his back. "Please!"

He glanced toward the bathroom door, then at her. "Just one thing."

"You're stalling!" she accused in a frustrated moan. "You're afraid to face it!"

"Yeah, that's why I became a vet. Four-legged creatures scare me." His expression was pained, as though he'd been injured. "What I was asking, Angel, was, is there anything *you* might be afraid to face—since I'm naked."

CHAPTER NINE

ALMOST EXACTLY twenty-four hours after coming face-to-face with Godzilla, Dana wedged herself in the pet door of her bedroom. She muttered, "Last night I was jumping into Sam's bed screaming 'man-eating dragon,' and tonight I'm stuck in a hole in a door. Interesting life!"

She twisted and tugged, but remained stuck. *"Drat!"* Too bad she couldn't call Sam to help her, but it was because of his suspicions her door was locked, and she'd decided to try to sneak out through the cat slot.

Her thoughts skittered back to last night, when he returned from doing battle with Dana's fire-breathing monster. Sam wore shorts she'd retrieved for him and around his neck was curled what he'd called "a very affectionate iguana named Agamemnon." Agamemnon was the daddy of the miniatures

219

Mona wore like brooches. Somebody had apparently left a door open somewhere, allowing 'Memo' to get utterly and completely lost.

Sam informed Dana she frightened the poor thing so badly, he'd slithered up to hide on top of her bed's canopy. The green beast that lovingly nuzzled Sam's cheek turned out to be barely three feet long, and embarrassingly fangless. Dana had felt stupid, but vindicated. At least Sam had to admit she hadn't made the whole thing up.

She tugged and joggled her body, but her hips raised painful objections to being forced through the cat door. She began to fear her escape would cost a pound of flesh. Okay, maybe five. "Come on, hips," she mumbled. "Sam's going to the nearest populated island tomorrow to call the coast guard. I can't—" she strained, yanking, and flinched "—let him!"

She had overheard Sam asking Beena if she'd told the supply boat captain about the malfunctioning satellite system. Beena's admission that she forgot rankled Sam. He asked his aunt if she'd really forgotten or if she were protecting Angel from the so-called border patrol. Beena just grinned. So Sam informed her he had to do something.

Not if Dana could help it! The time bomb of Tate's scheme was still ticking. This was Friday night—well, maybe the wee hours of Saturday. Next Wednesday was Tate's deadline. She had no choice but to hold Sam hostage for five more days. She squeezed hard, baring her teeth. *Rats!* She began to wonder morosely if he would find her stuck here in the morning like a size-twelve mouse in a size-ten trap?

Something sharp rammed her in the rear. Thanks to a reflex tensing of her gluteus maximus, her hips shot though the hole, and she sprawled on the hallway matting. She lay there for a minute, stunned. When her wits returned, she panicked. Had she screamed? She listened, afraid to breathe. The place remained dead quiet. After what seemed like a week, she felt positive Sam hadn't stirred, and raised up on an elbow to rub her perforated backside. There was something excruciating familiar about the indignity.

Peering at the pet door, she saw a little black nose and one yellow eye, peeping out over her ankles. ''Thanks, Pouncer,'' she muttered. ''Remind me to do something for you one day.''

Moments later she'd filched a penlight and screwdriver from Sam's desk, and crept to his boat. Quickly, she slipped through the man-hole-sized cover into the rear of the engine room. Five minutes later the twin engines were good for little more than bookends—until Dana opted to make them operational again. Dropping from the boat, she inhaled with relief. What a shame she had to pay for her security with overwhelming guilt.

She couldn't think about that now. She needed to get Sam's flashlight and screwdriver back in his desk, and then squeeze her backside through that dratted cat slot without being caught. She rounded the corner leading to Sam's office.

''Morning, Angelfish.''

Dana screamed, nearly jumping out of her T-shirt and boxers. Even caught in the act, Dana wasn't one to give up. She looked around blankly, made a show of blinking, pretending to see Sam for the first time. A candle flickering a few feet away made him easy to spot. He lounged against the clinic door, arms crossed over his chest. Clad in a pair of shorts, he watched her with a ''you're toast'' expression on his face.

Worse even, Beena stood next to him. She wore a pink robe, her lucky cat pin glittering on the lapel. ''I thought my aunt should see you in action,'' he said quietly.

She swallowed and placed a hand over her heart, concealing as well as she could the screwdriver she held. ''What—where am I?'' It was corny but it was all she had. ''What's going on?''

Sam's expression closed further. ''I was about to ask you that question.''

She stared, using her most befuddled look. ''I—I have no idea.''

"There, Sammy, love, you see?" Beena touched his arm. "She was sleepwalking!"

"Oh, sure." Sam peeled Dana's fingers back from her chest and plucked the screwdriver from its hiding place behind her hand. "With this?" He flipped it into the air, catching it.

"Why—I never saw that before," Dana said, grateful it was dark so her mortified blush wouldn't be detectable.

"Or this?" He snatched the penlight from her other hand with such a lightning-fast move, she jumped and gasped. Which probably didn't hurt her story, since she looked as startled to see the penlight as Beena. "These were both in my desk earlier today," Sam said.

Dana examined her hands as though seeing them for the first time, then looked up vacantly. "I wonder how I got them?"

Beena moved forward, taking her hand. "Sleepwalkers can do the strangest things." She faced her grand-nephew. "Sammy, love, I sleepwalk all the time. Why, once I woke up with a wire whisk in one hand and a shoe in the other. If Mr. Chan hadn't meowed and wakened me, I would have walked right into the kitchen freezer.'' She chortled. ''I'd have been a wrinkled old puny excuse for a Popsicle.'' She patted Sam's cheek. ''Enough of your naughty doubts. Leave poor Angel alone. She's had a terrible trauma. The poor child can't even remember her native tongue!''

Sam shifted toward Dana, his eyes igniting with exasperation. ''I'm not aware that sleepwalking is a characteristic of amnesia.''

Beena squeezed Dana's hand, fortifying her confidence. ''Maybe not in *dogs!*'' Dana said, jutting out her chin with bravado. ''But you're not a people doctor, remember?''

''Yes, Sammy, love.'' Beena pressed a kiss to her fingertips and reached up to plant it on his cheek. ''Off to bed with both of you. I'll hear no more of this silliness.'' She yawned and covered her mouth with her hand. ''Especially in the middle of the night. I need my beauty rest.'' She headed away from them, her bedroom slippers making a muffled skuff-skuff sound along the matting. Neither Sam nor

Dana reacted until the whisper of Beena's foot-steps disappeared.

Sam moved first and Dana flinched, expecting almost any act of violence. She knew he was furious. But when her glance snapped to him, he merely tucked the penlight and screwdriver into his hip pocket. "I'll put these somewhere safe." He took her arm. "I wouldn't want you sleepwalking with dangerous pointy objects. You could fall and hurt yourself."

She didn't speak, didn't look his way. Just allowed herself to be tugged along. When they reached her door, Sam glanced at her, then the pet entrance, then back at her. "I'll stay here to see that you get inside—safely."

After a moment when he said nothing else and made no move to unlock her door, Dana looked at him with reluctance. "Well?"

He indicated the cat door with a nod. "Go on."

She gaped. He didn't think she was going to chance getting her whopping huge backside stuck while he watched, did he? "You can't mean that I crawl in!"

"You crawled out."

She was startled he insisted she *crawl* in, so her expression was genuine, though the words were a lie. "I—I did?"

"Or you flew out the window."

"Well—maybe people can do things in their sleep they can't do awake."

"And maybe little green men from Mars beamed you through the roof." His jaw worked.

"Look, Doc, if I try to crawl through that thing, I might as well paint a bull's-eye on my backside."

A brow rose, indicating surprise. "No matter how badly you deserve a spanking, Angel, I don't hit women."

"So you *say!*"

His expression grew stormy. After a moment he dropped his hand into a slash pocket, drawing out a key. "I hope to hell that I'm not stuck here with my boat out of commission."

Her heart lurched. *He knew!* She faked mystification. "You're talking in riddles."

"In the morning my boat had better start."

She swallowed bile, but guarded the lie. Too many livelihoods were at stake to go soft now. "Are you leaving tomorrow?"

"Just a trip to the nearest populated island." His gaze searched her face, and Dana had the feeling he was trying to probe into her mind. "When I leave for good, have no doubts about it, you'll go with me," he warned. "So what about tomorrow? Will my boat start, or not?"

It was heartbreaking to keep silent. Sam's expression was bleak, his eyes glimmering with frustration and strain. The sad beauty clutched at her heart, making her falter. *No, Dana! No weakening!* "How would I know?" she snapped, her choices slim to none. "I— you're a crazy paranoid, you know that?"

For what seemed like an hour their eyes locked in open warfare, fighting a silent battle of wills. Anger and frustration thickened and heated the air, and breathing became painful. The instant Dana could no longer abide the tortuous silence, Sam broke eye contact. A curse on his lips, he unlocked her door.

"Understand this," he muttered. "Hurt my aunt in any way, and I *will* find you."

IT WAS DANA'S TURN to be suspicious. Sam had been down at his boat all morning, trying to get it to run. She stayed away, acting as if she had nothing to do with the fact that it wouldn't work. She'd expected Sam to show up with a big wrench in his hand and bludgeon her to death. But he hadn't.

However, he was doing something she hadn't seen him do before. He was crossing the lawn, heading toward the castle wall. But not in the direction of the beach, toward the interior of the island. Where was he going? Dana reclined on a lounge chair beside the pool, next to Beena and Madam Rex. The older women had fallen asleep and were snoring so loudly they'd caused cats to leap off nearby chairs and retreat to quieter locales.

Dana feigned calm, but she was as jumpy as…as—she couldn't think of a single cliché that fit. But she was plenty jumpy. She watched Sam clandestinely through lowered lashes, so when he turned her way, it looked as though all three women were sleeping. Dana figured the noise was so earsplitting, he'd have to assume all three of them were snorting and wheezing.

After he vaulted over the back wall, Dana was instantly on her feet, running. She didn't know where he was going, but she didn't intend to let him get very far from sight. He had to be furious and desperate. Those two emotions had a way of breeding a single-minded sense of purpose. She should know. Just look what her fury at Tate and her desperation to get away had fostered in her!

What if there were another boat on the far side of Haven Cay? Even with a little outboard, Sam could make it to another island. With a knowledge of the waters and enough anger, she bet he could swim there!

She scurried to the wall and peered over. He strode down the gradual incline toward the woods. Taking a deep breath, she scrambled over the barrier and dropped to the other side, recoiling from the pain to the bottoms of her feet. She started after him in a semi-crouched fast walk, planning to drop below the knee-high grasses if he looked back.

She was afraid she would lose him in the dense wood, but the path was relatively well-defined—a lucky break. She wasn't exactly Daniel Boone when it came to tracking. She crept to the far edge of a clearing in time to see him halt at the edge of a pond, twenty feet off to her left. With a suddenness that took her breath away, he shucked his shorts, and she gasped. He wore nothing underneath.

She covered her mouth, to stifle her out-burst. He was magnificent, poised there, all tanned muscle and—and so generously en-dowed. Any woman worth her X chromo-somes would have gasped. Dana's cheeks siz-zled and she prayed Sam hadn't heard her.

He stretched his arms above his head and plunged off the bank, executing a sleek dive. Dana sagged against a tree, relieved that she hadn't given herself away. She was afraid she wouldn't make a particularly brilliant spy.

Especially if it required watching great-looking naked men.

She shook herself, gawking as he swam the length of the pond, did a flip and began to swim back. Lord, he was a sight to behold. Her legs went mushy and she sank under the cover of tall grass and crawled toward the edge of the pond. She knew she was ogling, and that prying was not only rude but doubtless against the law. Much to her regret, however, she couldn't help herself. "That's probably what all the perverts say," she mumbled.

His route curved away from his starting point, but that didn't bother Dana. In fact it was a titillating stroke of luck, for he had veered in her direction. The water was clean and clear. As he neared, she witnessed the entire drama and beauty of his body in action, every supple component in concert with the others. She cupped her chin in her palms and smiled dreamily.

When he reached the side, she was too lost in the moment to realize he didn't flip and turn. Instead, he planted his forearms on the grassy bank, not two feet from her face, and rose up to eye level. Water dripped from his hair and sparkled on his lashes. He stared at the vegetation as though he suspected the yellow butterfly flitting in the grass wasn't the only creature lurking there. ''I don't mean to wake you, but what the hell are you doing?''

Caught off guard, Dana didn't know what to say. For an instant she thought he might be bluffing, but that fool's paradise didn't linger long. She grimaced, noting his blue eyes were wary, melancholy. The spectacle disconcerted her, and she could neither think nor run.

''Do you have other hobbies, Angelfish— *besides* sabotage and voyeurism?'' he asked quietly, ''or don't you remember?''

She made a pained face. *Drat!* Sam had heard her stupid gasp, after all! Her brain scrambled for any excuse. How was she going to explain—*yeeeeaaooow!*

Something painful goosed her forward. Instinctively, she grabbed for support. An instant later, she and whatever she grabbed hung suspended in cool, clear water.

Confused and disoriented, Dana opened her eyes. Her head smarted, as though she'd hit something. Sam's face was very near, and not quite in focus. He watched her, unblinking, his features somber, his hair slightly uplifted, wavy, as though in a gauzy, slow-motion dream.

Her arms were wrapped loosely around his neck. His slipped slowly, deliberately, around her waist. Deep silence and cool unreality prevailed in this place where gravity held little sway. She levitated there, drifted, floating her legs up to enfold his middle.

Their eyes locked in this hushed and weightless realm. Suddenly, they were no longer adversaries. Their guards melted away, replaced by an urgency as age-old as the sky, the sea, and the human desire to be joined, held—loved...

She felt herself flowing toward him, into him, pressing her breasts into his solid torso. His body tensed, his eyes widened. Dana intuitively recognized the need in him to cherish rather than conquer, to give rather than take, trust rather than doubt. Her reaction to this thrilling new wisdom was immediate and over-whelming. All the repressed passions within her shot upward and outward; her body ached to be one with his strength, his fire.

Their lips met softly, tenderly, a divine melding. Nestled within the haven of his body, their kiss deepened. Languidly, Dana opened her lips in invitation. It was so quiet, and no longer cool. She felt warm and peaceful and safe. Her eyelids fluttered and closed, and she wondered if this is what heaven was like.

Her consciousness began to dim as she yielded to a serene, hazy half sleep.

She experienced a vague sense of renewal and fought the cobwebs enveloping her brain. At first her lids were too heavy to do more than flutter. Then, some small part of her brain be-gan to perceive that Sam was breathing into her mouth. She opened her eyes, suddenly aware of his gift, nourishing her body and soul.

Her next few minutes were an inglorious mix of coughing and shivering, hunched on shore as Sam made sure she was alert and recovering.

"You have a bump on your head." His fingers smoothed her hair away from the stinging injury. "I'm sorry."

She hugged herself and leaned into his strength. "It's not your fault." She felt terrible about sneaking up on him, then ramming him with her head. "Pouncer and I are totally to blame." She glanced around for the kamikaze cat, but it was gone. Probably pretty satisfied with an assault well done. Dana inhaled, thankful her lungs functioned at full capacity, again. She nestled against Sam's shoulder. "How's your jaw?"

"Very hard." He nudged her chin, coaxing her to look at him. His expression held no amusement, but his lips tipped up slightly. She sensed it was because she'd stopped wheezing and gasping. "How many of me do you see?" he murmured.

"Still just the one." She turned into his neck and closed her eyes, comforted by the steady beat of his pulse. "I don't know what came over me,'' she whispered hoarsely. ''It's not like me to feel faint...'' She didn't know how to explain her near-blackout. She'd had worse bumps getting thunked on the head by falling library books. ''I'm so embarrassed.''

He put an arm around her. ''I should have brought you right to the surface, but I...''

When he didn't go on, she looked up. ''You—what?'' She already knew. She'd felt the same urge, but for some demented reason she needed to hear him say it.

His brow furrowing further, he watched her. ''I thought I saw...''

A kiss in my eyes? she finished silently, her smile timid. She knew it was insane, but whatever else happened under that water, one thing had been clear, to both of them. She *had* wanted Sam Taylor to kiss her. She'd wanted that kiss as she'd never wanted anything before. She'd wanted it so badly, she would have lingered over it with her last breath! Which she almost did.

''Sam?'' she asked, defying her natural timidity with men and allowing her desire for him to guide her. "I need to ask you something."

His expression was troubled, charmingly so. "Okay."

"Would you…" she faltered, afraid yet determined. This beautiful, naked man held her tenderly in his arms. He had saved her life, but gratitude had little to do with the tangle of emotions, desires and doubts that swirled inside her. She took his wrist. Taking a deep breath, she forbade herself to tremble as she lifted his hand to where his shirt was knotted beneath her breasts. "Undress me, Sam."

His long, dark lashes swept up in surprise.

SAM SAT at his office desk, his head in his hands. He was completely out of his everlovin' mind! First their little blonde mermaid had crawled up from the sea, claiming amnesia. Without tools or even clothes, she'd somehow disabled the radios, then managed to get him trapped in his storeroom to keep him from using the supply boat's radio. And finally, she vandalized his boat engines, essentially holding the whole island hostage, though nobody seemed particularly concerned about it but him. And what did he do?

He made love to her!

If that wasn't rockin' and rollin' his unstable butt right into a straitjacket, he didn't know what was. And the final insult? As they lay on a bed made of their clothes, sated and cuddling, she still looked him straight in the eye and lied. "What sabotage?" she'd asked. "What fake amnesia?"

He cursed, raking his fingers through his hair. Then, there was Liza to consider. *Damn!* Even though in his heart, he and Liza were no longer a couple, he still hadn't been able to let his long-time girlfriend in on that fact. No phone and no way off the island, had put a substantial stumbling block in his path. But the most hilarious detail about this whole crazy farce was that the *reason* he had no options in reaching Liza was due to the same designing woman he'd fallen recklessly in love with.

His chuckle was dark and ironic. It would be intensely educational to see just how big a fool he could be. He sat back, hauling in a breath. He had to get his head on straight. So he'd lost his mind for a minute and made love to her. So he'd fantasized for a few deluded moments—okay, more like sixty lusty, extraordinary minutes—that she wasn't *really* a bad person, that she had some plausible, understandable, even noble reason for doing all this.

"Hellfire and damnation, man!" He slapped his hands on his desk, vaulting up. "Get a grip!" He had to face facts—she was a siren. She lured him onto the rocks, and he was damn thrilled about it.

The rage in him billowed into a living, pulsating thing. He was incensed with himself. How dare he fall in love with somebody as deceitful as she? How dare his body betray him with her, knowing as he did, that there was no future for them? Knowing that beneath that beautiful, naive-blonde facade lurked a woman of wit, intelligence and sizzling sensuality—and a greedy, Machiavellian heart!

"Your good sense sucks, big time," he muttered.

"Sammy, love, is that any way to speak to the only woman in the world who would put up with such a non-whimsical grand-nephew?"

His head snapped up as his aunt pranced in. Though she was loaded down with rolled up newspapers clamped against her chest, her hands fluttered free. She flapped her fingers, as though drying her nails. Which Sam was sure she was doing, since her nails were so precious to her, the miniature cat art always changing.

"Here." She let the papers fall to his desk. "I don't want to smudge Mr. Chan." She held out her right hand, prominently displaying the index finger. "Look at that masterpiece! The head is tilted perfectly! I swear, Maya Angelou couldn't have done better."

"I think you mean Michelangelo."

She waved her fingers in a gesture that was part dismissing and part nail-drying. "Well, whoever. Madam Rex has outdone herself this time."

With an elbow, she nudged the pile of newspapers scattered on his desk. "I couldn't remember what part you wanted—cartoons or crosswords or the obituaries—no, that's Mona—anyway, I brought all the papers the supply boat left." She paused, looking confused. "Which part of the newspaper was it you read, again?"

"The news part." He tried to smile at his aunt, but the expression came with effort. Had it only been a few hours ago that he and Angel had been tangled in each other's arms, making crazy love...

He cleared his throat, snapping himself out of it. Dwelling on it would do nobody any good. "Thanks, Aunt Beena."

She blew him a kiss. "Dinner's in an hour," she started to turn away, then halted, scrutinizing him. "You look a little flushed. Are you feeling all right?"

He glanced uneasily around the room, then lowered himself to his chair. "I'm fine," he muttered. "Just—fine."

"Well, don't be late for dinner. I noticed you missed lunch. You and Angel." Her pause was long and meaningful. When he didn't hear her turn and leave, he looked up. She was grinning like the Cheshire cat. He frowned at her. "I'll be there."

She made a face, as though she wanted details and was irked that they weren't forthcoming. "Okay, I'll ask Angel where you two were during lunch."

"*Don't!*" he snapped, then wished he could cut out his tongue. "I mean, I'd rather you didn't say anything." Yeah, like bringing it up would make it real and leaving it alone meant it never happened? *Right, Taylor. You look good in denial.*

Beena's chortle filled the room. "There's no reason to be embarrassed, Sammy. I understand about honest passion, and I think she's charming. I couldn't be more delighted if I'd picked her for you myself. She's so much sweeter than that Liza Cold-Cut person."

He winced at the reminder, mumbling, "Colecutt."

Beena wagged her fingers. "If you ask me, that girlfriend of yours is full of *baaaa-low-nee!*" Beena turned away. "See you at dinner, love. And don't be late. You need your strength." She giggled behind her hand as she closed the clinic door.

Beena was more savvy than Sam had ever guessed. *Damn!*

Absently he picked up one of the papers and unfolded it. He glanced at the front page headlines, then flipped through the section. He felt as though he'd been stranded for a month. For all he knew, ten or twelve new political sex scandals had been uncovered in Washington, the stock market had roller-coastered through several more "worst" and "best" days in history, and, with luck, somebody had come up with a better place to store pollutants than our lungs.

He opened the editorial page and tried to pay attention to the words, but they blurred and ran together. With an irritated growl he flipped to the next section and froze.

Before him lay a photograph of Angel. Wearing a black strapless dress, she stood beside a tall, blond man, his arms wrapped possessively around her. Sam felt gut-punched and green-eyed jealous. Hesitantly, he scanned the caption. "Dana Lenore Vanover with her fiancé, Tate Fleck, on the evening before her mysterious disappearance."

The notion that Angel—rather, Dana Lenore Vanover—was a member of Miami's social elite had never occurred to him. Hope surged that he'd been wrong about her—his opinion having been tainted by the betrayal of the hired girl who turned out to be a thief.

His chest aching with the need to breathe, he scanned the society column. He hardly ever read it, the writer notorious for slinging mud and innuendos. But this was all he had.

He read. "'What's with Miami's wedding of the millennium, where the old name marries the new money? Though the dashing fiancé insists his lady-love is merely ill and incommunicado until her recovery, rumor has it the bride forsook the groom and is trolling for bigger fish—or at least a fish with a bigger wad.'''

Sam stirred uneasily in his chair, rereading the last sentence. After going over it a third time, he slumped back and rubbed his temples. *Lord.* His worst fears seemed to be confirmed. She had the name but no more money, so she'd decided to get back in the fast lane-any way she could.

It was strange that her fiancé, this Fleck person, insisted she was ill, and not missing, since she clearly was. Sam assumed the lie was a pride thing. Maybe Fleck thought he could find her and get her back without adverse publicity. That made sense. The men who came by on the boat were no doubt friends of the groom. Sam had to admit, he'd probably have done the same thing in Fleck's position. Losing a woman like—Dana—wouldn't go down easy.

It looked as though Miss Vanover decided, at the last minute, that marriage was too confining. Why not con a daft old lady out of a few million and still be footloose and fancy free!

Ice spread through his veins. He didn't want to believe it, but... *"Hell!"* He'd known it! He'd felt it all along. So why did his heart feel like winter-kill?

He bowed his head.

Because you love her, stupid.

CHAPTER TEN

DANA WAS SICK at heart. How could she have asked him to undress her, of all crazy things! What of her vow to look into a man's soul? Oh, she'd done a lot of looking, and feeling, and sighing with Sam—even some outright moaning—but none of it had had much to do with searching his soul. She quivered with the delicious memory of his hands on her, his lips—his gentleness.

How could she have let herself go like that, in his arms? It must have been the head injury. Or she'd been more affected by lack of oxygen than she'd thought. What was with her? Having sex with Sam Taylor was about as wise as walking barefoot over a pile of glass shards. Did she think she would come through the experience without spilling blood?

She bit back a sob. She was in no position to be falling for any man. Her heart had been battered and was in no shape to take chances. She couldn't trust her own feelings—not after the Tate debacle.

What she and Sam shared had been a rebound thing, nothing more. She had to recognize it as that and get herself under control. Besides, practically every second of their relationship had been based on lies and tricks. Sam didn't trust her. He might fancy her a little—the mysterious stranger fantasy—but nothing meaningful could come from it. He could never be positive of a word that came out of her mouth.

She'd avoided him since that disaster at the pond on Saturday. Or had he avoided her? Did it really matter who avoided whom, as long as it worked? She'd eaten every meal in her room, explaining that she had a terrible migraine. Beena seemed to think this was a good thing, and came by periodically to shout through the door, words like *taco, adiós, olé* and *que sera sera,* which Dana suspected was Italian. However misguided and inexact

Beena's efforts, her concern was well-meant and endearing.

Dana adored the elderly sprite, and couldn't bear being the lying hostage-taker she was. She spent Sunday gazing blankly out the window or sprawled on her bed, crying. She came to depend on the cats for company and comfort as they wandered in and out. After an hour or two of being snuggled and slobbered on, they escaped to nap in peace.

Sam knocked several times, insisting he needed to speak with her. She repeatedly pleaded that he go away. Today, he wasn't taking no for an answer.

"Please, Sam!" she cried as evenly as her despondent mood would allow. "I'm not feeling well."

"It's Monday morning. If you still have a headache, you need a doctor. Let me in."

"I'd think you'd be happy I'm staying in my room," she called. "I can't *steal* anything in here!"

He didn't immediately respond, and she held her breath, hoping he would go away. She was afraid to see him. Afraid to see anger in his eyes—eyes that could be tender, could drink her up, make her feel clean and new and special.

So here she sat, a prisoner of her own lies and longings, defeated and miserable.

"Dana," he said grimly, "let me in."

She lay on her back, her mind exhausted, without hope. "No, Sam, there's nothing..." She frowned, her brain insisting that she quit wallowing in guilt and self-pity and *think* for a minute. What had he called her? Dana? She lolled her head from side to side, denying the notion. She was more fuzzy-witted than she'd thought.

She heard the rattle of a key and sat bolt upright, tugging her T-shirt snugly over her hips. "Don't you dare!"

The door cracked open; she could see his face, angular, handsome. Deep shadows darkened the skin below his eyes. He looked as if he'd had less sleep than she. "I know who you are," he said. "Dana Vanover."

She stilled, tried to swallow, but her throat was dry. "What did you say?" *How could he know?*

He stepped inside and closed the door. "It was in the paper."

"What?" She hadn't had much rest, but she didn't know she was so far gone she couldn't handle the meaning of simple words like "paper" and "it" and "was" and "in" and "the." But they confused her, didn't make sense.

"The supply boat brought last week's Miami newspapers." He held out the article with her picture. "Tell me that isn't you."

She stared. Yes, she remembered the news photographer who'd been on the yacht snapping pictures that night.

The jig was up, it seemed. She flicked a glance at his face, so solemn, so dear. "You're right. It's me."

"Admit you never had amnesia." His voice was more afflicted than angry.

She exhaled, not sure she was sorry she'd been found out. It had been a hard, cruel secret to keep. "You're right. I never did." She shifted to sit on her feet, wadding her fingers in her lap. "But—" Her heart turned over with a wayward need to hug him, beg his forgiveness, and for him to make love to her again. But she resisted. "I'm so sorry for all the lies, but I—I can't explain. Not yet."

He frowned at her, blinking with astonishment. *"Why?"* He asked the question with such incredulity, it was as though she'd said she had no choice but to set her hair on fire.

She shook her head. "After Wednesday everything will be all right. After Wednesday, I can go home." She dropped her gaze, unable to look into those tormenting eyes. "And so can you."

He moved to the edge of the bed and knelt, gripping her by the upper arms. "What are you saying, Angel—*Dana?* Why have you pretended to have amnesia? Why did you screw with the radios and my boat? What's going on, damn it?"

She peered at him from beneath her lashes, wanting badly to tell him everything. Wanting to wipe the distrust from his eyes. Wanting him to take her into his arms, kiss her, make tender love to her again. But that was a selfish fantasy. She couldn't trust him. She couldn't trust anybody. Not even herself, it seemed. It was impossible to fall in love with someone when the whole relationship was based on lies. Wasn't it? And even if it weren't impossible, she'd blindly allowed herself to trust someone she'd loved before, and that had ended badly.

At least she'd thought she loved Tate. Yet what she felt for Sam—out there by the pond—*Lord,* what she experienced in his arms, was so much more profound than anything she'd ever felt for Tate.

"I—please, Sam. Just two more days," she pleaded. "Trust me."

She knew what his reaction would be. A nasty laugh and a cynical retort. When he didn't immediately speak, she grew more and more uneasy. She knew he was watching her. He still held her arms, but his grip wasn't painful.

"*Trust* you?"

Her glance shot to his face, to eyes displaying the rueful luster of skepticism. "Trust *you?*" She watched a gamut of emotions cross his features. "That's very..." He squinted, peering around the room, as though he needed a moment to reorient himself. When he faced her again, his gaze caught hers and held like a vise. He stared, clearly wishing he could reach inside her mind and drag out the truth. "All right, Dana," he finally said, his voice solemn. "I'll trust you."

She stared, tongue-tied. She hadn't expected this. She'd expected outrage and sarcasm. But he didn't sneer, or smirk, or even glower. He just watched her with grave, glorious eyes that seemed to inquire, *Are you going to deceive me?*

She shook her head, a mute vow. She had no words. A shuddering thrill danced through her and she experienced a lightness in her heart she hadn't known in...in *forever.* After all she'd done to him, he'd promised to trust her. She was so grateful, she wanted to cry, to fall into his arms, but she didn't dare. She was beyond tears, drained of them. And falling into his arms would be a reckless indulgence.

He released her and stood. ''I may be the world's biggest fool...'' He started to say more, then frowned and shook his head, as though arguing with himself. ''I'll be ready to listen when you're ready to tell me.''

Dana nodded, bewildered by his manner. It seemed almost as though he...but that wasn't...especially, not after everything....

Mystified, she watched him leave the room.

AFTER LEAVING DANA in her room, Sam was at his wit's end. He'd gone over the article more times than he could count. He couldn't think logically anymore, couldn't sleep. Absently he went into his room and lay down on the bed. He closed his eyes, but his mind churned.

A light knock on his bathroom door startled him. ''Yes?''

''It's me.'' She sounded calm, perhaps resigned. He sat up in surprise. ''Dana?''

He heard a click, and shot a glance toward the handle in time to see it move. After only a brief hesitation, the door opened slightly. She stood there, looking tired. She'd changed into a bright mauve-and-yellow-striped shirt and pink shorts. One of Beena's more gaudy tie-gifts threaded through the belt loops, cinched the shorts at her waist. Her hair was slicked back in a ponytail. Sam noticed she wasn't wearing the ruby drop she'd won at Beena's birthday party. As a matter of fact, he'd never seen her wear it since Beena had placed it around her neck at the party.

"Could we walk on the beach?" she asked.

He nodded, and jumped up as she opened the door enough to join him. She didn't speak or look at him, not even when he took her arm. He knew body contact wasn't a great idea, but he needed her touch. He needed to inhale her subtle fragrance. He'd been a starving man for nearly two days. He'd eaten, but wasn't nourished. Hunger gnawed all the time, deep in his belly. It was a hunger that nothing and no one but the taste, touch and scent of Dana Vanover could slake.

In silence, they walked out of the castle, across the manicured lawn, through the stone arch and over the undulating dunes.

The shrill call of gulls winging overhead and the hiss of surf were the only sounds that broke the quiet. Sam waited, trying to let her open up to him in her own way, in her own time. Lord knew, he'd waited for what seemed like an eternity already.

"Sam?" She halted and faced him. "I want you to know, I had no choice in what I did. I couldn't afford to trust anyone." Her brow creased and she looked out to sea. "You see, I trusted Tate with all my heart, and he—" Her voice broke and she shook her head, plainly trying to get her emotions under control. "Anyway, I didn't know you. I didn't dare hand over the power to give me away."

He didn't understand. Give her away? Though he wanted to believe her, he tried to discipline his mind. He was afraid, because he loved her, he might jump at any explanation she came up with. He needed to know she was telling the truth. Even if it was a truth he didn't want to hear. "Why don't you start from the beginning?"

They walked along the water's edge, away from the dock, as she quietly and sometimes brokenly told Sam the story of the whirlwind romance, of Tate's charm and charisma. These things were hard to hear, but he kept his own council and let the words spill out of her as she chose to release them.

Dana told him about discovering that she and her mother were pawns in a scheme, requiring Tate to marry a respectable old Miami name. Their marriage would legitimize his ploy, sucker unsuspecting investors. Tate would then grab a fast fortune before he disappeared, leaving Magda and Dana to deal with the scandal.

"So you see," she said, tears glistening in her eyes, "I had to get away. I jumped off the yacht and swam and swam for hours—until I washed up here." She swept out her arm. "I thought I was swimming toward Miami. I didn't have any plans. But when I realized how perfect a place this island was to hide…'' A tear trickled down her cheek. She paused to get her voice under control. "I was desperate, Sam." It came out in a faulty whisper. "I'm sorry."

He wanted to believe her. Nothing she said conflicted with the newspaper account. But it was so…so Hollywood. His cynical inner voice reminded, *She's lied so much, how do you know this isn't another trick to get your sympathy, to pull you off your guard?*

"Can you prove any of this?" he asked, wishing he could sweep her into his arms and tell her he believed her, tell her he loved her and wanted nothing more than to show her how much.

She blinked, shooting him a startled-fawn expression. "I—no. That's the reason I had to hide. I can't prove any of it. Tate has powerful friends. I…" She shrugged, looking small and helpless. "You don't believe me?"

He experienced a surge of compassion, but it failed to erase his doubts. He didn't know if he could get past all the lies. How crazy was it to love a woman, yet require *proof* that her every move, thought, or act wasn't choreographed to hurt or swindle?

"You don't believe me." She chewed on her lower lip, frowning and pensive. "I deserve that." She took both his hands. "Every word is true, Sam. Honestly."

He frowned, his heart battling with his head. "Dana…"

He heard a sound, and glanced toward the sea. A sleek sport fishing boat headed toward their dock. Someone waved and called out from the flybridge. He couldn't make out the words, but the woman looked familiar. He squinted. "Liza?" The realization hit so quickly he hardly grasped the fact that he'd spoken her name aloud.

"Who's that?" Dana asked.

His gut clenching, he pulled from her grip and waved. "I only recognize one of them."

"They're coming *here?*" Panic edged her words.

"Looks that way." He peered at her. "Should I fear for their equipment?"

"This isn't a joking matter." She anxiously stuck a stray wisp of hair behind an ear. "Tate has until the end of the workday, Wednesday, to do his sleazy deal. I put my trust in you, Sam. Please don't betray me!"

"I won't," he promised in a whisper.

The boat slowed, pulling up to the dock. The woman was definitely Liza. She no longer waved or shouted, just watched. Sam had a feeling his jealous soon-to-be-ex-girlfriend was weighing the situation, wondering about the pretty blonde. He glanced at Dana. "You'd better go."

"Hey, Sam, *honey!*"

He faced the boat and grinned. "Hi, Liza." Without looking at Dana, he whispered, "*Go.* I'll get rid of them." He waved, loping toward the pier.

He had no clue why he was protecting Dana. *Hell, he knew, all right!* He just didn't like to think about it while being scrutinized by the woman on the boat. To call Liza merely obsessive was like calling Shakespeare merely a man who scribbled words on paper. Sam and Liza had their biggest fights after she'd surprised him at work, accusing him of giving some female pet owner too much attention, which was a crock. But her jealousy was part of her makeup, and he'd learned to deal with it.

He bounded onto the dock, a very unhappy man.

She scrambled down from the flybridge and jumped onto the wharf, running into his arms. ''Darling!'' She kissed him with all the over-compensated ardor of a women with a ''Who's the bimbo?'' look in her eyes. ''I've missed you, honey! I thought you were coming home Friday. I tried to call, but couldn't get through. What's going on?''

Sam took her by the shoulders, moving her slightly away. He needed space. His heart was no longer in their relationship, and he saw no reason to try to put it back. But he had to let her down easily, and this wasn't the time nor place. ''Nothing's wrong. Just a radio snafu.''

He glanced at the boat, not recognizing it. "Who are your friends?"

She resisted being held away from him and snaked her arms around his neck. "I was about to ask you the same question," she murmured against his mouth. She indicated the direction of the castle. "Who's the blonde?"

Here it came. Liza's no-nonsense, scratch-her-eyes-out method of handling every situation that included Sam and any female over the age of consent. Unfortunately, in this case, Liza would definitely have a case. "She's a guest of my aunt," he said.

"A young, pretty guest." Liza's suspicions were apparent, even masked beneath a facade of purring and rubbing. "Weren't those a pair of shorts your aunt sent you for your birthday last year?"

Hell! She recognized the clothes. When a woman had on a man's shorts, it was pretty damning, even in a trusting woman's mind. With all the incriminating evidence at hand, he and Dana might as well have been rolling around naked on the beach screaming, "Yes! Yes! Oh, *baaaaaaby!*"

How did he explain the fact that Dana had crawled out of the sea, practically naked. And for days and days she'd worn his clothes completely platonically. Since that was no longer the case, he opted for a lie. "You're mistaken. Those were hers."

"And the tie?"

Good Lord, the woman had the eyes of a spy satellite. "She forgot her belt?" He didn't like the way that came out.

"Come on, Liza!" a man wearing a backward baseball cap shouted from the flybridge. "Tell him to get a move on."

Sam peered at the boat. "Is he talking about me?"

"One second, Amos!" she called. "Go help Andrea mix the bloody Mary's. The fish aren't going anywhere." She turned back and smooched Sam's jaw. "Honey. The Sawyers invited us to go deep sea fishing, so I said yes." She reached up and twisted a breeze-tossed lock of his air around a finger. "You need a day off."

He had no intention of leaving the island. Not that he didn't believe Dana's story, but he couldn't allow himself to—not completely. Not yet. He didn't intend to set a foot off Haven Cay until Dana went with him. A voice deep in his head whispered, *And you hope like hell when that happens, she'll leave as your fiancée.* "You know I hate deep sea fishing, Liza," he said, trying to sound reasonable. "I keep wanting to patch up the fish and throw them back."

She made a pretty pout. "Not even to be with me?" Liza was a delicate beauty, with willowy Audrey Hepburn looks. Even her black hair was cut short and pixie-like. Though she had lovely eyes, she added fake lashes, and she emphasized her full lips with a thick pencil line, making her mouth appear puffy. He knew balloon-lips were the latest trend. Why that was baffled him. Yet, even with the unnatural additions that annoyed more than aroused, Liza was hard to say no to.

He decided to lie again, realizing with some irony that lies did have a way of cutting troubling corners. "I have to perform surgery this afternoon." He knew Liza well, and though he needed to get things settled with her, it would be cruel to break off with her abruptly after all they'd been to each other. "I'm shorthanded in the clinic. I could use an assistant during the operation. Why don't you stay?"

She pulled a face. "Gag me, Sam! I can't stand that stuff. Can't you put it off?"

"I'm afraid not. You know how my aunt is about her cats."

The brunette's brows dipped. "Insane?"

He smiled wryly. "Now, now. She's my only family."

"Oh, Sam," she said, looking put out, but doing it prettily. "If you have one *big* flaw, it's your loyalty and duty to that old lady. If you ask me, it's pathological!"

"I owe her a great deal, Liza," he said. "You know that."

"Let's not fight, honey." She smiled, and he could tell she was reloading her arsenal of reasons he should go with her. "I haven't seen you in so long."

"I know." Once again he took her by the shoulders and pressed her slightly away. He had no desire to be unkind, but he didn't feel right about playing a game his heart wasn't in. "Since this isn't a good time for me to leave, you go fishing with your friends. I'll be home Wednesday evening—I'll call you. We need to talk." He winced. That had come out sounding more portentous than he'd intended.

Her eyes narrowed slightly.

"Hey, Liza!" the man shouted. "Get a wiggle on, babe!"

Sam flicked a glance toward the boat. The man waved a glass, sloshing something red.

"One minute!" she shouted, then turned to Sam. Tilting her head back, she peered into his face. "Okay, honey. I'll go." Her smile was a little thin. "But first, I have something to tell you."

Her tone told him she didn't intend to be put off. With a stab of irritation, he manufactured a grin. "Sure, what is it?"

"This is hardly the way I pictured it, but…" Her features brightened with enthusiasm, mixed with a hint of something else. Sam couldn't quite make it out.

He experienced a prick of foreboding.

Foreboding?

The idea was so stupid he shook it off.

Hugging him to the familiarity of her slim, toned body, she whispered, "I'm pregnant, sweetheart!" She kissed his jaw. "It's time we set the date."

DANA PEEKED OUT from the castle's double doors, watching the exchange on the dock. She watched Sam kiss the slender brunette, watched the intimacy of their body language, the significant smiles. A terrible sense of loss assailed her. She felt sick, and clutched the door to keep from slumping to her knees.

She hadn't wanted to face it, but the truth hit her like a cannon shot to the stomach. She was in love with Sam. She even knew when it happened—under the water, in his arms. He may have given back her life with his breath, but he'd stolen something equally precious.

Her heart.

Watching him and his lady, Dana's misery became a biting, physical ache. She loved a man who couldn't trust her. Couldn't believe her, even after she took him into her confidence and revealed a perilous truth. A man who clearly had a very close relationship with this Liza person.

Sam helped Liza onto the dock, and she headed toward the boat, throwing him a kiss. He turned away, toward the castle. Dana wondered if he told her to notify the coast guard. She shuddered, clutching her hands to her chest.

But what if he hadn't? She felt a swell of hope. What if he cared enough for her to trust her, even after all she'd done? What if he loved her? She'd had the strangest feeling when he'd visited her room today. And there had been something in his eyes out there on the beach. She watched him as he approached, a small smile twitching at the corners of her mouth. In her woman's heart she knew he cared for her. He couldn't have made love to her the way he did if it had been nothing more than a conquest.

She looked past him as the fishing boat accelerated and motored off. Maybe Liza *had* been his girlfriend, but that was in the past now. It had to be! Dana felt that so strongly she wouldn't allow herself to believe otherwise. She was so certain she had trusted him with her heart and her secret. Sam was honorable, like her father. He was nothing like Tate. No power on earth could make her believe he was!

When she glanced back at him, he was mounting the stairs. She opened the door and stepped out, but the smile on her face died. He wore a stony mask of cold dignity, a watchful fixity in his eyes.

''Sam?'' Unable to stop herself, she took his hands. ''What is it?'' She sensed it couldn't be the guilt of betrayal, for she knew in her heart he wouldn't give her away. She knew so much in her heart, now that she'd finally made a clean breast of everything. "What happened?"

He squeezed her fingers, his faint smile haunted with sadness. "Congratulate me, Dana," he said. "I'm getting married."

The shock held her immobile for a moment. Grief overwhelmed her. Perhaps he hadn't betrayed her secret, but...

She had no right, no reason, to feel betrayed. He'd never made her any promises, never even whispered words of love. After all, she'd asked him to make love to her, hadn't she?

Still, in her shattering despair, she did feel betrayed. He cared for her! No—*he loved her!* She knew it as surely as she knew he hadn't informed on her to the coast guard. "This...this is sudden," she said, fighting the need to scream, *Why, Sam? Why her and not me?*

His nostrils flared. "It was time." He pulled from her grasp, but she felt his reluctance to do so. With a distracted gesture, he indicated the door. "I need to get back to Miami, but

I'll stay until Wednesday evening. Can you have the boat repaired by then?''

Her fingers tingled with the memory of his touch, and she clutched her hands together. ''Uh, it won't take long.''

''What about the radios?'' He was all business as he opened the door for her to precede him.

''I can fix the satellite, but yours is blown.'' She faced him, her mind reeling, her body an insubstantial mess. ''I'm sorry about that. Please, send me the bill.''

His jaws working, he didn't glance her way.

''So...so when is the happy day?'' she asked, unable to help herself.

''Soon.''

She nodded, but he didn't see, for he was walking away from her.

CHAPTER ELEVEN

SAM FELT DEAD INSIDE. He went through the motions of working in his office, but he couldn't feel. What had he done, promising to marry Liza? He held his head in his hands. He loved Dana, yet...

So what if he had a strong sense of duty? That wasn't all bad, was it? He owed Liza a great deal, and he cared for her. Even if his sense of duty really was pathological, he'd taken four years of Liza's life, he'd had sex with her. He'd conceived a baby with her. And until Angel—Dana—came along, he'd been content with her as the woman in his life.

When he looked into Liza's eyes out there on the beach, all he could think of was Beena and how she'd been cheated out of her wedding day. So he promised Liza a wedding. Just as soon as she could arrange it. Maybe he'd been rash; maybe he'd been foolish. Nevertheless, he'd promised.

Very likely, once he got back to Miami, this whole episode would seem more like dream-like lunacy than reality. Some crazy outbreak of summer dementia brought on by a silly obsession with a beautiful, mystery woman who'd crawled out of the sea. Any man might get a little confused under the circumstances.

He didn't know if he believed anything he was telling himself. But for Liza and their baby, he would try.

WEDNESDAY AFTERNOON, Dana ran into Sam in the hallway. She had hardly seen him since Monday, which she considered a blessing. It was difficult to be around him, under the circumstances. No matter what else had happened between them, Dana knew no one on the island would betray her, so she had taken the metal earring piece out of the satellite cable and it was working again. Five minutes in the engine room yesterday repaired Sam's boat.

''Hello,'' she said, trying to sound placid.

He flicked her a glance, and she stared into his eyes against her will. She was almost physically staggered by the frightful reserve she saw there. It hurt. And it also made it clear that she had built up very little unbreachable resistance to him over the last two days.

"Can you be ready to leave after dinner?" he asked.

She nodded. "Of course, I have no luggage."

He looked away, his jaw muscles working. "Right."

"Around seven?" she asked, her heart crying out to say more, so much more.

He nodded, flicking his glance back. He opened his mouth to speak, but quickly clamped it shut, merely nodding.

"Sammy! Sammy, love!" Beena's anguished cry pierced the air, and they both turned to see her fly around the corner toward them. Even from a distance Dana could see tears stream down her face. "My lucky brooch!" she sobbed. "It's gone!"

Dana was keenly aware of Sam's scrutiny. She faced him, startled to see a flicker of assumed betrayal in his eyes. Betrayal? If anyone had been betrayed, it hadn't been Sam! She stiffened. ''You can't believe I took it!''

''Of course we don't believe any such thing, Angel.'' Beena grabbed her hands. ''It's just that the pin is a keepsake from someone very dear to me. I can't bear to lose it.'' Distraught, she clasped Angel to her, crying against her shoulder.

Dana's glance clashed with Sam's. ''You can frisk me if you want.''

He kept his expression under stern restraint. ''If you insist.''

She blanched, stunned.

Beena waved a hand. ''Don't be silly, Sammy!'' She choked back a wail. ''Let's look for it. I'm sure the clasp gave way. I should have allowed a jeweler to check it to make sure it wasn't in need of repair. *It's all my fault.''* The sentence trailed off in a moan.

Sam coaxed his great-aunt away from Dana, and with a protective arm around her, began to lead her toward her room. "You rest, Aunt Beena. I'll get the staff on it right away." He peered at Dana. "I'll see you in your room."

"I can't wait!" She lurched to her room, feeling bereft.

When Sam arrived thirty minutes later, she threw her arms wide. "Let's get it over. Strip search me."

He came inside and closed the door. "I intend to."

A blush crept up her neck and burned her cheeks, but she held her stance. "Go for it! Pervert!" This was so wrong! They'd gone full circle in their relationship. Once again, he didn't trust her. *Period.* And she was calling him names. Suddenly it was all too much to stand. Tears welled in her eyes, and he blurred in front of her.

She loved him. *Loved him.* He didn't trust her, and though she felt he cared for her—even if those soft feelings were against his will—he was marrying another woman. Tilting her head with bravado, she battled to staunch her weeping, but it was no use. One traitorous teardrop after another escaped and slid down her face.

His blasphemy cut through the heavy silence. "Just be ready to leave at seven."

A moment later Dana was alone.

WITH A GAPING HOLE where her heart used to reside, she said a tearful goodbye to Beena, and climbed into Sam's boat for the return trip to Miami.

Though Beena was still distraught about the loss of her cat pin, she was happy Dana had regained her memory, but not quite convinced she wasn't a refugee. She made Dana promise to write.

Of course, this was another lie Dana was forced to tell to appease the older woman. She knew Sam would never allow an association between them. And, in truth, Dana didn't want one. She wanted—needed—to be completely severed from any connection with Sam. For her heart's sake.

The trip back to Miami was made in awkward silence. Dana knew Sam cared for her.

Yet, for his own reasons, he chose to betray them both with his decision to marry Liza—a betrayal more devastating than anything Dana could have imagined enduring at Tate's hands.

The sea grew rough. Deep in the night, under a sky full of stars, Dana was tossed into Sam's arms. The moment was bittersweet, and she feared the memory would rest uneasily in her heart for a very long time.

At the marina, they parted without words.

CHAPTER TWELVE

"OUCH!" Dana wagged her scraped knuckles. One thing she'd never been very good at was changing the water pump in her old clunker. She always, *always* scraped her knuckles.

And her back hurt. Cringing, she bent farther beneath the hood and gave the pump a dirty look. "It's you or me, buddy. And I'm betting on me!" She applied her wrench again, then stilled. Something on the radio caught her attention. "My—goodness," she murmured. The reporter said Tate Fleck, along with several high-ranking city officials, were under indictment for fraud. She inhaled a shuddery breath. Vindication, at last! Perhaps her mother would stop looking at her with that pinched expression, and be grateful she wasn't embroiled in a full-fledged scandal.

And maybe Sam would...

Shut up, Dana! she told herself. *Sam is out of your life.* She hadn't seen any announcement about a wedding in the paper—not that she'd been obsessing or anything. But it had only been three weeks. Planning a wedding took time.

She hoped Beena had found her brooch. It would have been nice of Sam to let her know. She bit her lip. Maybe Beena hadn't found it! Maybe he still believed she was a thief. "So, why haven't you sent the police to search my place?" she muttered. "If you're so sure I—*aaaaaaoooooooch!*"

The jab in her backside made her bang her head on the hood. With both her cranium and her rear throbbing, she staggered around to slump against her car. "What was—"

Stars danced and whirled around in her garage. She squinted, trying to make out what else was there that hadn't been a minute ago. Pouncer? And—and... *"Sam?"* Backlit by the late afternoon sunshine, he stood just out of reach. Her heart reacted wildly. Even dressed in slacks and a knit shirt—more clothes than she'd ever seen him wear—she marveled at how he could possibly be more handsome than she remembered.

He walked to her and picked up the cat, holding it toward her. His smile was breathtaking, yet his eyes were watchful. ''Pouncer was despondent after you left,'' he said.

Too stunned to form words, Dana accepted the kitty.

''I was, too,'' he added softly. ''No matter what I told myself.''

Pouncer meowed and leaped from Dana's arms onto the roof of her car. Dana hardly noticed. Sam was too what? She opened her mouth, but nothing came. It was hard to remain composed and rational, being so close to him, even when she wasn't suffering from a concussion.

''Dana,'' he said in a husky whisper. ''I was miserable without you.'' Very slowly and gently he took her into his arms, as though giving her time to break and run. ''I wanted to believe you. In all honesty, I did. I was just— I had other problems…''

She frowned, confused. He was apologizing, she could tell. So Beena must have found her brooch. But that didn't change anything substantially. He was still marrying another woman. She tried to say it, tried to tell him to take his hands off her and get out of her life, but her brain had gone all dopey. She had the thinking capacity of mush. She had a feeling the blow to her head didn't have much to do with it.

He scanned her face, his smile disappearing. "I love you, Dana. I've loved you from the first minute I saw you." He pressed his cheek against her hair, his lips brushing her ear. "Let's start over—forget everything—all the lies and doubts."

He held her close. She could feel his heart. Racing. Pounding. Hardly the heartbeat of composed indifference. She pulled back to stare into his face, dazed and dizzy. Unspoken hope shimmered in his eyes along with a breathtaking sadness.

"Dana?" he asked, frowning. "Don't you know me?"

She swallowed, shaking herself out of her stupor. ''Aren't...aren't you an engaged person I used to know?''

He shook his head. ''Not anymore. Liza told me she was pregnant. She wasn't. I guess, when she saw us together on the beach, she sensed how I felt about you and decided...'' He shrugged, the action weary. ''When she faced the fact I was marrying her out of duty, she broke down and told me the baby was a lie.''

Dana saw the irony and smiled sadly. ''It seems you've been beset by several lying women lately.''

He kissed her on the forehead. ''Please— let's forget all that.'' His kisses trailed to her cheek. ''Marry me, Dana.''

She closed her eyes, allowing the precious request to penetrate to the marrow of her bones. Her heart spilled over with joy, so much so that she couldn't hold back a husky laugh.

Sam lifted his head, his expression unsure. Uncertainty in a man as imposing as Sam was endearing. Her heart soared to heights she had never even dreamed possible.

Touching his face lovingly, she teased, "You want me to marry you, even after I scammed Beena out of Pouncer?"

His expression softened as he glanced at the cat, contentedly grooming itself on top of the car. "Beena found her brooch," he said.

"Of course, she did."

Sam's gaze returned to Dana. "It dropped off in a cereal box. She almost ate it."

"You don't have to explain, Sam."

"Yes, I do," he said, contrite. He ran a hand lovingly over her face and through her hair. When he inadvertently touched her bump, she winced.

"Oh—darling," he murmured. "I'm sorry."

Darling! He called her darling! An overwhelming sense of contentment engulfed her. The man she loved, loved her back. What in life could be more perfect than this one, wonderful miracle?

"I'd better examine you," he said, worry glimmering in those heavenly eyes. The sight was so galvanizing it sent a quiver of longing through her. A longing, she realized, she no longer had to deny.

Slipping her arms around his neck, she placed a butterfly-light kiss on his jaw. "I think you're right, Doctor. You should examine me." Her kisses moved gradually to one corner of his mouth. "Very..." She kissed the other corner, detecting a slight upward quirk. "Very..." Her mouth brushed his. "Very thoroughly—darling."

And to her everlasting delight, he did.

**MILLS & BOON® PUBLISH EIGHT
LARGE PRINT TITLES A MONTH.
THESE ARE THE EIGHT TITLES
FOR MARCH 2002**

———————— ❧ ————————

RAFAELLO'S MISTRESS
Lynne Graham

THE BELLINI BRIDE
Michelle Reid

SLEEPING PARTNERS
Helen Brooks

THE MILLIONAIRE'S MARRIAGE
Catherine Spencer

EMMA'S WEDDING
Betty Neels

PART-TIME MARRIAGE
Jessica Steele

MORE THAN A MILLIONAIRE
Sophie Weston

BRIDE ON THE LOOSE
Renee Roszel

MILLS & BOON®

Makes any time special™